# THE COFFIN MAKER'S BOOK OF DARK TALES

# PRAISE FOR CURTIS M. LAWSON AND JOSHUA REX

"Gorgeous and gutting, visceral and inventive, Joshua Rex and Curtis M. Lawson have done something truly singular with *The Coffin Maker's Book of Dark Tales*. Rex's inimitable literary style and talent for imbuing his stories with dread that builds like a crescendo is perfectly paired with Lawson's ingenious, haunting storylines and layered (often tortured) characters. A dark delight unlike anything on your bookshelves."

—**Christa Carmen, author of**
*Something Borrowed, Something Blood-Soaked*

"As reader/book reviewer I have spent the last 4 years mining the depths of independent and small press horror. I have found many, many gems, but none as flawless as Curtis M. Lawson and Joshua Rex."

—**Well Read Beard**

"Lawson is a representative of the contemporary evolution of cosmic horror. Post-Lovecraft, post-Ligotti, but cut from the same strange cloth."

—**Laird Barron, Author of *Swift to Chase***

"Lawson is not merely a rising star in contemporary weird fiction… he has fully arrived and is a force to be reckoned with."

—**S. T. Joshi**

"Curtis M. Lawson is a formidable new talent in the horror/weird fiction scene, soon to garner more well-deserved attention for his riveting and wildly imaginative work."

—**Jeffrey Thomas, author of *Punktown***

"… (Lawson's) characters are beautiful, intense disasters."

—Horror Novel Reviews

"Joshua Rex continues to demonstrate why he is one of the most dynamic young writers in the weird fiction field."

—S. T. Joshi

"Rex' writing is poetic and stylish…"

— John McIlveen, Stoker nominated author of *Hannawhere*

"Here's the thing about the works of Joshua Rex. Though the words on the page look like prose, they read like poetry, like music, like raw emotion. Though Rex calls himself a writer, he's also an artist, a historian, the tall, gaunt Ghost of Lives Forgotten."

—Heather Miller, author of *Knock Knock*

"I am left both astounded, and yet envious, of Joshua Rex's talents."

—Tylor James, author of *Beneath the Jack O' Lantern Sky*

"*The Coffin-Maker's Book of Dark Tales* is a classic to be long heralded and treasured by all fans of dark and weird literature."

- Barry Lee Dejasu, author of
*Dark City Skylines and Darker Horizons*

# THE COFFIN MAKER'S BOOK OF DARK TALES

Curtis M. Lawson
& Joshua Rex

WEIRD HOUSE

ISBN: 978-1-957121-28-4

Text © 2021 by Curtis M. Lawson and Joshua Rex

The New Governess was originally published by Bloodshot books in Not Your Average Monster Anthology, 2015.

Cover and interior art © 2022 by Luke Spooner

Editor & Publisher, Joe Morey

Interior and cover design by Cyrus Wraith Walker

Weird House Press
Central Point, OR 97502
www.weirdhousepress.com

# CONTENTS

# ILLUSTRATIONS

# THE NEW GOVERNESS

I make boxes in the anthropoid shape. The old woman you're about to meet carries around boxes too — they're slightly different in form but for equally as gruesome a purpose. And what to say about the wicked, privileged little brats in this story? Only that they're about to meet their match in their latest governess, one Mrs. Gertrude Peals.

Unlike the hapless women who have previously held the position, Mrs. Peals is prepared for everything Harold and Lucy have planned for her, and may reveal herself to be more creature than teacher...

# THE NEW GOVERNESS

They had succeeded in getting Miss Sims sacked the same way they had Miss Hilary: by being naughty to the point of evil. Sims had been Harold's victim. It had only taken five weeks—a record! The rat, bagged in the pantry and snuck under her sheets as she slept, had been the final indignity. She was gone the next morning, without notice and without collecting her pay. When confronted by their parents, the Lord and Lady Ashton, the children feigned innocence, proclaiming their most recent governess to be uneven in temperament, and to be sure, a bit barmy. They alleged to having seen her licking the condensation off the windows of their lesson room (which wasn't true) and writing endless letters to a certain deceased gentleman (which was) instead of instructing them in Greek and piano.

It had been a thrilling month, but the following week was rainy, dismal, and decidedly dull without Miss Sims to harass. So, Harold and Lucy were ecstatic when their mother informed them that a Mrs. Gertrude Peals would be interviewing for the open position the following morning. During breakfast, one of the servants announced the candidate's arrival.

"Show her into the red parlor, Caster. Tell her I will be with her shortly," said Lady Ashton.

After they had eaten, Harold and Lucy crouched at the closed drawing room doors, excitedly pushing one another out of the way to get a glimpse through the keyhole. Beyond, they could hear their mother droning on and on about the history of the house. A voluminous fern partially obscured the interviewee where she sat, but the children could see the hems of a grey skirt, varicose ankles, and wooden shoes.

"She's an old woman!" said Harold. "You got an easy one, Lucy. You should have her broken within a week."

Lucy hushed him. "Shhh! I think she's about to speak!"

"You come to us with little in the way of references, Mrs. Peals. However, I understand that you were briefly tutor to the Maisten children?"

Harold and Lucy looked at each other. Neither was smiling now.

"Indeed, my lady," said Mrs. Peals. Her voice was low and grainy, with an odd wheeze. After a moment she added: "A regrettable tragedy. They were a lovely family, if you don't mind me saying so."

"Truly. As you might have supposed, we were acquaintances of the Maistens, given our proximity to Arlington Park, or what's left of it. Lord Maisten was a hereditary peer like my husband. I've heard the ruins are still smoldering." Lady Ashton paused and slowly sipped her tea. "Were you present at the time of the fire?"

"I was away, unfortunately. In London."

"Actually, I'd say you were *quite* fortunate," Lady Ashton said steadily.

"I must respectfully disagree, my lady. The past month has been dreadful. I've lain sleepless many nights since. The tender faces of those children are all I see when I close my eyes."

"And what of your family, Mrs. Peals?"

"I am widowed. My husband's been gone twenty years now."

"And no children of your own?"

A considerable pause.

"I wasn't able."

"I see."

"Might I ask how old the children are?"

"Harold is twelve and Lucy nine. They can be quite ... unruly at times. We've had three governesses in the last nine months, all of them young ladies. To be plain Mrs. Peals, his lordship and I have reached our wits' end. The children need stern guidance and firm reassurance, someone compassionate towards them, yet ... unyielding. I believe an older, more mature woman of your experience is better suited to demand obedience while simultaneously nurturing their intellectual development. Is this a charge you are willing and able to assume?"

"Indeed, your ladyship."

"Then it is settled." Lady Ashton picked up a gilded bell, rang it thrice, then folded her hands imperially in her lap. "Caster, show the children in."

Behind them Harold and Lucy heard footsteps, then were draped in a long shadow. Caster was tall and solid, with a dark and craggy face and a thick swathe of tightly-groomed red hair. The children despised him; he was the only servant they had not yet succeeded in intimidating (he was far too clever for their tricks). He also had an advantage: he'd been employed at Langston House thirty-two years, working up from footman to butler to their father's valet. Now, he glared down at them with his customary palpable distaste.

"Shall I open the door, or would you prefer to continue spying like imps through the keyhole?"

Harold rose and emphatically brushed off his pants. "I would *prefer* it if you performed your duties without insolence."

"Yes, mind your own business, Caster," said Lucy dismissively.

"Perhaps we might begin afresh with this one, and find other ways in which to amuse ourselves," he said as he turned the knob.

Harold and Lucy strutted haughtily into the chamber, but when they saw the old woman they froze as if they'd just walked into a den where something dangerous lived. Mrs. Peals sat at an angle from their mother, broom handle-straight in her chair, wooden heels crossed primly, her gnarled hands folded in her lap. Her hair was like layers of gossamer web, spun into a tight bun. A hideously potent and decidedly old-fashioned floral *eau de toilette* wafted off the woman and permeated the room. Her clothing was impeccable, though drab and aged. She wore a billowy blouse and a long grey woolen skirt, both of which appeared at least thirty years out of date and emitted a decided mustiness. The portrait on the cameo at her throat was odd and grotesque, the silhouette resembling a withered head.

"Ah! Here they are. Children, this is Mrs. Peals, your new governess."

The old woman's neck creaked as her head slowly swiveled in Harold and Lucy's direction. She wore strange rectangular glasses with mirrored lenses and her teeth were the same color as the stuff Harold had once seen come out of a cricket he'd smashed.

"Is she blind?" Harold asked his mother.

"Harold! How incredibly rude," said Lady Ashton.

"It's quite all right, my lady," Mrs. Peals interjected. "It is an obvious peculiarity about which I am often asked." She looked at the children; Harold and Lucy saw themselves like a pair of dolls reflected in the lenses. "My eyes are extremely sensitive to light, young sir. The mirrors reflect the majority, allowing only that which is in my periphery to penetrate."

The Lady Ashton looked suddenly concerned. "But your vision is otherwise sharp?"

Mrs. Peals' gaze remained on Harold and Lucy. "Perfect."

0

The new governess brought with her only a pair of black trunks: one small and old, the other large and new. The children watched from the drawing room as she carried the small trunk up the stairs, trailed by a pair of footmen who brought the larger box to the little garret on the fourth floor where all the Ashton governesses had lived.

Later, Harold and Lucy were outside in a shallowly wooded area of young trees flanking a creek that ran through the estate property. They liked to go there to discuss matters of the house out of earshot of the omnipresent Caster. Lucy was rocking back and forth on a large bowed vine threaded between two trees and watching Harold as he poked through the brush and decaying leaves with a large pointed stick, looking for something to hurt.

"So, what have you planned for the unlucky Mrs. Peals?"

Lucy paused in her swaying. "I haven't decided."

Harold frowned. "Lessons begin tomorrow! You know that the first day is always the most crucial, especially as this one seems … different. She'll be harder to break."

"I thought you said she was 'just an old woman', that she'd be 'easy?'" Her brother didn't respond. Lucy recommenced rocking on the vine. "She's very strange looking. Do you think she's a witch?"

Harold laughed. "Don't be stupid."

"What do you make of those spectacles?"

"You heard her. She can't see in the daylight."

"That's not what she said."

"Well, it's all the same."

As Harold overturned a rotted log a toad sprung out. Suddenly exposed, it leapt in the direction of the water and safety, but Harold deftly pinned it down with the stick and held it there, grinning as he watched it struggle under the point, which he slowly pressed into the toad's soft belly. The little creature's movements became frantic, its arms and legs jerking. The stick passed through it with a *pop*; Harold held up the impaled the creature, still spasming, for Lucy to see.

"It's dancing!" Lucy laughed.

They watched it die, then Harold flung it against a tree and went back to searching along banks.

"What if she started the Maisten fire? You don't think she could have, do you Harold?"

"No."

"What if she's lying?"

"Why would someone burn down the very house where they are employed? Some ham-fisted maid probably knocked over an oil lamp."

"Yes, you're probably right," Lucy said. She swung off the vine, gathered a handful of stones along the bank and began skipping them in the creek. On a low branch to her left she spotted a bird's nest filled with hatchlings. Harold picked up some rocks as well and joined in. They succeeded in knocking the nest out of the tree, sending the squawking chicks into the water. The mother bird flew in suddenly, cawing and screeching above her drowning lot. Lucy brought her arm back and winged her last stone, hitting the mother in the head. The bird froze midair, then plummeted in a spiral of limp feathers into the creek.

"Well struck!" cried Harold, clapping her on the shoulder.

Lucy beamed back at him.

0

Lucy lay in bed for hours that night, going over a mental list of tricks: salt in the old woman's tea; a spider down her shirt; a nasty rumor about something illicit between her and Caster …

*She'll be harder to break*, came her brother's voice. The words appeared in Lucy's mind as if illuminated by a lantern, and with them came at last an idea. She slipped out of bed, crept down the hall to the butler's pantry and took a small bottle of lock oil off one of the shelves. Lucy pulled the stopper, picturing how she'd pour it in a discreet place somewhere behind the governess's table. *She's old … the fall might kill her*, Lucy thought, and stood for a moment, considering this. Then she re-corked the bottle and started back to her room, grinning.

*Oh,* then *how proud Harold would be!*

0

"So, what awaits our new friend Mrs. Peals? Something *wicked* I hope?" Harold was sitting with his fork in his fist, tines up like a rebellious peasant as he waited for his breakfast to be served.

"Oh, it is wicked indeed," said Lucy.

"So, what is it?"

Lucy told him.

"Brilliant!" he said, with a mischievous grin. "We must eat quickly in order to set the trap. I have a feeling that this one rises early ..."

The servants set down their plates. Harold raked scrambled eggs into his mouth while Lucy nibbled on a toast point, too excited to eat anything more. Ten minutes later they were hurrying down the hall to the lesson room, Lucy fingering the phial of oil in her pocket as they approached the door. But when they opened it their cheerful expressions faded; the governess was already there. Mrs. Peals stood in the well-lit room like a statue with her back to the free-standing blackboard. The early morning light reflected in the mirrored glasses like coins over a dead man's eyes. The old woman was wearing the same clothing as the previous day, and the rancid floral scent pervaded the space. She held a thin white baton like a wand with which she pointed at a pair of small desks and said sharply: "Sit." Harold and Lucy glanced at one another, then moved toward their respective seats.

"We will begin today with a lesson in the science of anatomy," said Mrs. Peals stepping away from the blackboard. Pinned upon it was a stunningly life-like illustration of a flayed man. His chest was butterflied and the organs beneath were neatly labeled. He was nude and completely shaven except for his beard and the hair on his head, and all of his intimate details were on display: the penis cross-sectioned; the scrotum cut open to reveal the design of his testicles. Lucy blushed and looked away. Harold frowned and cocked his head.

"This is a rendering of a deceased male, aged thirty-one," Mrs. Peals began.

"This is *ghastly!*" Harold exclaimed.

"Children will *not* speak out of turn, Mr. Ashton," the governess snapped.

Harold's nostrils flared. "*You*, madam, are to address me as *Master* Ashton."

Mrs. Peals came toward him, her wooden heels like gavel blows on the floor, and stopped at the edge of his desk. Harold saw himself reflected, fish-eyed, in each mirrored lens.

"You are a child, Mr. Ashton," Mrs. Peals said, her voice like an ominous buzz. "Children are masters of nothing, save error. As your elder I am your superior in this classroom and in all matters besides, therefore I shall be accorded with the proper respect at all times, is that understood?"

For a moment Harold only stared, his mouth open, his face a conflicted mask of affront and fear.

"*Is that understood,* young sir?"

In a small and rather boyish voice, Harold replied: "Yes, Mrs. Peals."

Lucy regarded this exchange with unmitigated awe. Miss Rudy had been the last who had attempted to chastise her brother. Harold had responded by hitting himself in the eye with a doorknob and claiming that she'd struck him, and Miss Rudy was gone before tea the same day.

"Continuing, then. This drawing details the remains of a man who perished in so-called peak health when ... *yes*, Mr. Ashton?"

"Pardon the interruption, Mrs. Peals," Harold said, "I was only wondering how the man died?"

"He drowned. Note the slightly swollen larynx and the burst capillaries along the walls of the lungs ..."

Harold squinted at the rendering, his eyes following the baton as Mrs. Peals circled the areas on the dead man's throat and chest.

Lucy raised her hand. "Why are you *showing* this to us, Mrs. Peals?"

"So that you might gain a better understanding of the workings of the human body, madam."

"But we are not medical students, and that man is, well, *exposed*," Lucy said. "This is scandalous! Father would have us whipped for merely speaking of it!"

"There is no indecency in science," said the governess flatly. "It is a man-made notion which exists solely to establish behavioral boundaries in society. In truth, we are no more than animals going about in slacks and sashes, and *your* meat is no different than *their* meat. A pound of flesh weighs the same, no matter its origin."

"What is that yellow object near the man's stomach?" Harold said.

"That is the pancreas, an endocrine gland that produces important enzymes which aid in digestion," said Mrs. Peals.

The anatomy lessons continued the next day and the day after that, without a single Greek letter or minuet note appearing alongside the Latin names for organs and tissue and the 206 bones in the human body. The subsequent charts grew more grotesque as well. On Monday of the following week, Mrs. Peals produced one of a murdered woman. The body was scored with slashes and chops. Each wound was labeled according to its severity, with one in the throat and one in the abdomen marked FATAL.

At the conclusion of these lessons, Harold would become irritable and sometimes violent. In the great hall he would meticulously set up his thousand-strong army of toy soldiers in epic battle maps, only to kick them over in a fury or crush them in his fist like some merciless god. Lucy tried to get him join her in terrorizing the maids, but Harold increasingly had little enthusiasm for anything except Mrs. Peals' macabre lessons. And along with Harold's bad temper, Lucy's anxiousness increased. It wasn't so much the drawings of human cross-sections and dissections anymore that distressed her, but rather the way Mrs. Peals grinned greyly when Harold got the answers right.

One morning as they arrived for lessons Harold and Lucy found Mrs. Peals waiting for them with her small black trunk standing with its lid open on the table before her. "Thus far," she said, "I have relied on diagrams to illustrate the lecture material. Today we will be examining some actual specimens."

Lucy's heart began to gallop as the governess reached in and brought out a jar in which something grey and angular floated, and set it on the table.

"Do either of you know what this is?" Mrs. Peals asked.

Harold raised his hand.

"Yes, Mr. Ashton."

"It's a shark!"

Lucy squinted at the grey object floating in murky fluid. It was indeed a shark. The pewter-colored dorsal fin was small but distinct, as were the rows of arrow teeth just visible through the A-shaped mouth on its ivory-white underside. The eyes were opaque, with a faint dash of cold blue at the center, and the tail, designed for pulsing thrusts through the sea, lay curled and useless against the bottom of the jar.

"Correct, Mr. Ashton. It is an infant *Prionace glauca*. A tiny predator, unaware of its lethal capabilities."

She went back to the trunk and took out another jar, this one much larger, and set it next to the shark. At first glance it appeared to be filled with knotted clumps of black hair, but as Mrs. Peals turned the jar a face came into view. Jagged vertebra stuck out from its severed neck, propping the head up off the bottom of the jar so that its right cheek rested against the glass. The eyes were half closed, the flattened expression mournful. It was too furry, its features too pronounced, to be human. Lucy had only seen photographs, but she recognized the oversized lips, large square teeth and the tawny, wrinkled skin stretched over broad cheekbones.

"It's an ape," she said gravely.

"Very good, Miss Ashton. A chimpanzee, to be specific."

"Did you kill it, Mrs. Peals?" Harold asked.

The old woman laughed, a sound like a saw raking across wood. "No, not I, Mr. Ashton."

"Well, whoever did made crude work of it," said Harold, half rising out of his chair to get a closer look.

"Indeed," said Mrs. Peals. "An early attempt—a ... *rehearsal*, shall we say."

The instructor took out a third jar. This one contained a human baby's head. It was completely white, and the top of its skull had been removed so that the brain was visible. At the sight of it, Lucy's stomach lurched dangerously. She stumbled away from her desk, ran from the room and into the hall where she vomited onto the glossy marble floor, as well as on her father, who happened to be passing through. He glanced at his soiled shoes, then glared at Lucy.

"Father, forgive me," she sobbed. "It was Mrs. Peals' fault! She showed us something *awful!*"

Lord Ashton's eyes narrowed on the lesson room door. He started toward it with Lucy on his heels like a scolded dog. But as they entered, Lucy found a very different scene. The jars were gone, the lid of the trunk shut and the latter nowhere to be seen. Now there was only a chart featuring a dissected cat pinned to the board. Harold, scribbling notes, stood when he saw his father. Lord Ashton looked at the picture, then Mrs. Peals, his stony expression fixed.

"What subject is this, madam?"

"The science of anatomy, my lord."

"For what purpose?"

"My intent is for the children to obtain a clear picture of animal physiology."

Lord Ashton paused, eyeing the pen and ink rendering of the innards.

"Well, perhaps you might utilize examples less visceral? Those which will not render my daughter physically ill?"

"Certainly. I shall make the adjustments."

Lord Ashton turned and left the room, shouting for Caster. Lucy watched him go, reluctantly, before turning back in her seat. Harold was staring at her.

"I'm disappointed in you, Lucy," he said. "I thought you had a stronger stomach."

Mrs. Peal was staring at her too, as was—or so it seemed—the desiccated face in her cameo.

0

The following week, the Lord and Lady Ashton departed for London on the invitation of His Royal Majesty to attend the Prince of Wales' engagement gala. Mrs. Peals had three days previous taken sick, and so the children were left to their own distractions. It was overcast and dreary, with periods of intermittent rain, so they stayed inside most of the time. Lucy played with her dolls until she couldn't stand them anymore and decided to go looking for Harold. He'd been cold to her since the incident with their father, but she wanted to talk to him about Mrs. Peals while the old woman wasn't lurking about. She found him on a window seat in the library, staring at the black clouds hovering wraith-like above the estate's bright green lawn. He didn't acknowledge her as she sat down across from him.

"What is it, Lucy?" Harold sighed impatiently.

"What if mother and father find out?"

"About what?"

"Mrs. Peals. About what she's *really* teaching us."

Harold looked up at her and blinked in a slow deliberate way. "Why would they find out?" There was an edge to his tone which made Lucy pause and choose her next words with care.

"What if Caster's been listening in?"

"Ha! Caster ..." Harold scoffed. He leaned back into the nook and threaded his fingers behind his head. "The only place he's been snooping is the wine cellar. You know, I caught him tapping the Madeira last week. I've got him in my pocket now. One word of it to father and he'll be banished from this house forever."

"But doesn't she *frighten* you?"

"Mrs. Peals? No." Harold gazed out the window where the cloud grumbled and crackled. "On the contrary, I find her quite intriguing. She's not like the others. Her lessons actually *matter*."

"Well, I *am* frightened. I think I'm going to tell mother what's been going on."

Harold suddenly shot forward, grabbing his sister by the braids. She squealed, but Harold pulled harder; she cried out, he pulled harder still.

"You won't, Lucy! You *won't*, do you hear me?"

"*Harold!* You're *tearing* it—"

He pinned her down with his knee on the crimson window seat cushion. His teeth were bared. The rain began, striking the library windows like a volley of arrows.

"You won't say anything to mother *or* father, will you Lucy? *Will you?*" he screamed.

"No! No! I *promise!*"

Harold suddenly released her and settled leisurely back into the cushions again with his hands behind his head. Across from him Lucy whimpered, wiping shamefully at the tears on her rouged cheeks. Harold hadn't bullied her that way in years, and she had come to think of them as equals—associates in their malevolent games. But in a flash, he had reasserted himself as the Older Brother, a *man*, like her father—a figure to be Feared and Obeyed. Gradually she composed herself and began fixing her braids as the rain hammered the leaded panes.

"What do you find so fascinating about her?" Lucy asked.

Harold thought a moment. "She doesn't think me wicked."

"Neither do I."

"No," Harold sighed. "But *you're* just a child."

Lucy felt herself begin to cry and ran from the room before her brother could see her. In the entry hall she found Mrs. Peals, hunched and limping across the dim corridor toward the staircase. Her gait was crooked and dragging, as if she had little control of her legs. She held in one hand a small glass bottle and in the other a candlestick. The taper stub dripped wax onto her hand, but the old woman did not flinch. The little flame illuminated her sagging, mottled face and the limp hair that hung like torn cloth. *She looks ill indeed … like death*, Lucy thought. Then: *Why is she downstairs?*

To spy, she realized—on her and Harold. Emboldened by this perceived impunity, she marched down the hall, beckoning the governess with all the haughty, aristocratic authority her nine years could muster.

"Mrs. Peals, haven't you been instructed to *remain* in your room when not teaching us?"

The governess stowed the bottle in her robes as Lucy approached. She paused at the newel, arrested not so much by Mrs. Peals' appearance as the cloying reek of her perfume, which seemed to have been applied liberally in order to disguise something rank. She wasn't wearing the cameo, and up through the gap of her unbuttoned collar stuck a small black thread. Lucy eyed it curiously, then set her eyes, in the best imitation of her mother, on the governess, giving the old woman the same stern look the Lady Ashton offered the servants when she was cross with them.

"What is that you have? Something you've *stolen*?"

There was a long pause; then, slowly, Mrs. Peals leaned in close, her body creaking and groaning as if lowered by ropes and pulleys, until the girl was looking directly at her own frightened reflection in the mirrored lenses.

"I know what troubles you, child. You fear that I am attempting to come between you and your brother. That *I* am the reason for his recent distance. You do not understand that he is guided by his own instinct. Learning, you see, is as much intuition as instruction. It is the recognition of one's own nature, and the subsequent laboring to bring it to fruition. Harold comprehends this; he knows the dark color of his heart. But not you … you struggle with what you are, like one kicking at the walls of her own house."

Lucy took a step back. "No, it's *you*. You are corrupting him. Ever since you came, he has been different."

"I am only a catalyst, child—giving water to the weeds of thought so that they might flourish."

"You and your *lessons* are ghoulish and uncouth, and I am going to tell my mother and father straight away when they return," said Lucy primly, though she was trying to control her shaking as she moved around the old woman and started up the stairs.

"And what would big brother think of you then?" Mrs. Peals called after her. "How will he react when he learns *you* were the one that tattled? That had me removed from my position?"

Lucy stopped, turned back. The old woman was grinning at her, her teeth the color of tallow in the taper light.

"I've said all, Mrs. Peals. The next time you see either of us will be from the window of the carriage after your dismissal."

Lucy steadily mounted the stairs, but the moment she was out of sight she ran—down the hall to her room where, for the first time in her brief life, she drew the bolt.

0

The next day Caster went missing. A maid had gone to his room when he had not reported for breakfast service. After much knocking and beckoning, she tried the door, found it unlocked, and entered. Everything was immaculate, and his things were still therein; he, however, was not. The contention was that he had unexpectedly gone to town on some urgent business. But as morning turned to afternoon and finally evening, concern became dread. The house was searched from the servant quarters to the outbuildings but neither Caster nor any trace of him was found.

During all the commotion, Lucy was looking for Harold. He was at breakfast, but then had gone off somewhere and she hadn't seen him the rest of the day. Their mother and father wouldn't return until the following evening, and as night fell, moonless and rainy, Lucy began to feel very frightened. It occurred to her she hadn't seen Mrs. Peals since their encounter the previous night on the stairs. Since the old woman was ostensibly "unwell," no one had disturbed her during the search for Caster. An unsettling intuition told her where she might find her brother. With dread enveloping her like a cloak, Lucy climbed the stairs in the semi-darkness towards the fourth floor.

A door opened and closed above her as she gained the third-floor landing. Lucy hid in a gap between the wall and a grandfather clock, holding her breath as a figure slowly came down the stairs. It was Harold. He was walking slowly, trance-like, his face blank and his skin so pale it glowed like a ghost in the gloom. There were copious amounts of dried blood on his shirt cuffs. Lucy peeked around the clock, glancing first in the opposite direction to make sure Mrs. Peals hadn't followed, and whispered: "Harold! ... *Harold?*"

Harold continued catatonically down the stairs and disappeared below; a few moments later she heard his bedroom door open and then close. Lucy was starting after him when a loud thud from the floor above stopped her on the stairs. Harnessing her fear, she climbed to the uppermost landing and crept along the wall in the cloistered darkness towards Mrs. Peals' door. As Lucy approached, she heard the clinking of glass and the sandpaper scratch of lids being unscrewed. She knelt in front of the door and looked through the keyhole.

Centered in her line of vision was a long wooden table. The small black trunk stood atop it with its lid raised. Beside the trunk was a white wash basin full of steaming water; a line of empty glass jars without lids; a long-handled spoon, and a spool of thick black thread stuck with a needle. Mrs. Peals was bent over, getting something out of the large trunk on the floor. She rose, turned, and set it on the table. Lucy, somehow, managed to arrest the sharp little girl scream that tried to escape.

She could only see the object from the back, but immediately Lucy recognized that flame of hair, now damp and tousled and sticking up like the feathers of a shot bird. She'd never seen a hair on Caster's head out of place before, and the sight of it was somehow almost more disturbing than the latter being no longer attached to his body. Mrs. Peals had her arms out, searching for something—a short wooden chair which she pulled up to the table and sat. Lucy could see her full on now. The old woman's face drooped like melted wax; her teeth were like rotten piles stuck in mud. Mrs. Peals brought the head closer, turning it so that it literally faced her, and gave it a pat as if it were an animal she wanted to stay put. The mirrored glasses reflected the blazing fireplace. The governess brought her hands up slowly and removed them.

Lucy gasped—Mrs. Peals was staring back at her through the keyhole. But something was wrong with her eyes. The whites were grayish and the pupils, dark and misshapen, were coated in a thick opaque glaze. When she looked down at the head, only the right eye followed her command; the other slid left, then rolled toward the ceiling. Mrs. Peals blinked several times, then stuck her fingers into her left socket and pulled out the roaming eye. It made a noise like a cat vomiting as it came away in her hand. She plopped it on the table, then picked up the long-handled spoon and, digging her nails into the scalp to steady the head, scooped out the left eye and popped it into her own empty orbital socket. She did the same with the right eye, then closed her lids and opened them again. At first it was all whites; then, very gradually, Caster's olive irises rolled into view.

Mrs. Peals tossed the head in the fire and went to the small trunk.

The sound of glass jingled in the room like lively piano music as she pulled out several jars filled with assorted organs, along with a large beaker of blood. She set them on the table beside the empty jars and unscrewed the lids. Then she rose, unbuttoned her blouse and pulled it back off her shoulders so that it remained tucked into her skirt but hung like a tattered apron around her waist.

Lucy cringed. The body beneath was emaciated. The skin was blotchy, the color of boiled chicken, and the breasts hung to the sides like desiccated leather strops. There was a long black zigzag down the center of the old woman's chest, ending in that peeking thread Lucy had glimpsed earlier, jutting like a worm from her throat. Mrs. Peals pinched this now and pulled. The opening began to gape; a smell like the breath of Death wafted through the keyhole. Lucy covered her nose and mouth with her skirts in haste. Mrs. Peals coiled the grimy string on the table, put her fingers inside the slit up to the knuckles. The ribcage swung open like a pair of well-oiled doors. It looked like a fire had raged through the governess's insides. The organs were shriveled shadow masses and the lungs flapped and rattled with her breathing like pierced balloons. She transferred the organs, starting with the lungs, next the liver and kidneys, then continued to the other viscera, alternately dropping the spent ones in the clean jars and rinsing her hands in the white basin before inserting the fresh organs. When the transfers were complete, she picked up the large jar of blood, feebly brought it to her lips and took a few slow sips, grimacing at first, but then drinking feverishly, draining the beaker nearly dry before setting it back on the table.

Of the rancid organs, all that remained now was the heart, tiny and black, like a beating chunk of coal. Mrs. Peals sat again, stuck her hand into the fetid cavity and grasped it. The heart struggled like a tiny animal in a trap, beating quicker and quicker but then sagging and almost liquefying as it came away in her hand. She dropped it in one of the empty jars, a black smear streaking the side of the clear glass, and rinsed her hand in the steaming basin. Then she plucked the fresh one from the jar and inserted it in the other's place. But the new heart didn't beat, it just hung from the arteries like an over ripe fruit, and the old woman slumped sideways in the chair and went still. At length, the new heart twitched, thumped irregularly a few times, shuddering at first, then becoming stronger until it was throbbing steadily.

Things began to change.

The veins swayed snake-like as the blood flowed, turning everything grey-black but pulsing and vibrant, a dark forest coming alive with terrible magic. Mrs. Peals' outer appearance was changing as well: her drooping jowls lifted; the crooked teeth formed tight ranks once again in the gums; the black splotches on her skin faded and then vanished altogether. The old woman seemed to snap awake, drew a long gurgling breath and closed the ribcage. Then she took up the black spool and sewed the skin back together, the needle finding the well-worn holes with little difficulty. Afterwards, she dressed and pulled her hair back, silver and lustrous again and with an oily shine in the firelight, and began the task of disposing of the dead organs, tossing them in the flames and rinsing the jars in the basin before replacing the lids and returning them to the small trunk. The smell of the burning, rancid meat made Lucy involuntarily wretch, and with it escaped the tiniest involuntary cry. Mrs. Peals looked at the door like a cat about to strike. She put the glasses back on and stealthily slid around the table, her movements now eerily fast and fluid.

Lucy ran, cringing as her footsteps reverberated through the corridor like a drum. She turned around only once as she was rounding the corner. Half-illumined by the garret firelight, Mrs. Peals stood in the hallway, watching her.

◊

Lucy went straight to Harold's room and beat upon the door until he opened it. His eyes were red and wet, and for a moment he seemed to not recognize his sister.

"What do you want, Lucy?"

"Harold let me in," she hissed. "*Quick!*"

Harold frowned, glanced past her down the hall, then moved aside just enough for her to enter the room and shut and locked the door.

"What did she make you do, Harold?" Lucy asked.

A long pause. "It doesn't matter. He was already dead."

"How do you know that? Is that what she told you?"

"He had a heart attack, Lucy," Harold stated. "He died in his bed."

"Maybe he did, or maybe *she* killed him. I'm almost certain it was poison. Either way, she made you cut him up!"

"Since when are you so fond of Caster?" Harold said. He tried to put an edge on his words, but his voice cracked instead.

"Harold, she's a monster!"

"What are you talking about?"

In a low voice, Lucy told him what she'd seen.

"You're mad," Harold whispered, looking away.

"I *saw* her do it with my own eyes and—" Lucy broke off, not wanting to say it, not wanting to admit she'd been caught. Harold angled his head slightly and frowned.

"What?"

"She saw me."

Harold swallowed.

"We have to leave," said Lucy. "Even if just for the night. We'll come back when mother and father return tomorrow evening."

"And where will we go, Lucy? The woods? The village? Where would we sleep?" Harold asked, on the verge of crying again.

"There's a cave on the other side of the creek," Lucy said. "Remember the one we found last summer? We can sneak out the back in the morning before the servants rise."

"How will we know when mother and father have returned?"

"There's a good view of the northern road from the spot."

Lucy got up and started toward the door. Harold grabbed her arm as she passed.

"Where are you going?"

She looked down at him, noting how terror had reduced the tyrannical Older Brother to a puling little boy. "To gather food. We'll need something to eat if we're to be gone all day."

"I'll come with you," he offered weakly.

"No, you stay here. I will only be gone a minute or two—just to the pantry and then to my room for my cloak. I think we should sleep in the same room tonight."

"Yes," Harold said with a relieved sigh. "I was thinking the same." Then, as Lucy reached the door, Harold said: "I'm sorry I pulled your hair."

Lucy smiled fleetingly, then slipped out of the room and silently hurried down the back steps toward the pantry. There, she filled a wicker basket with bread and jam and fruit and a pair of mincemeat pies along with some linens and a bread knife. She carried all this back upstairs, gathered her cloak and boots from her room, and then returned to Harold's. He propped a chair under the doorknob and then the two of them got under the covers. They didn't put out the candle.

0

Lucy woke as dawn was graying the windows. Rolling over, she stared at the empty pillow beside her for a second or two, and then shot up in the bed. The chair was cast aside, the door ajar. She rose, grabbed the bread knife from the basket, and cautiously peeked into the hall. She did not see Harold, but she knew where she would find him. Filled with a great foreboding and a frenetic feeling of dread, Lucy crept up the stairs to the fourth floor. The door to the governess's garret was opened; a soft, cold light penetrated the otherwise black corridor. For a long moment she stood mustering her courage, then peered around the door frame.

The room, to her surprise, was empty, save for the rude table and chair, and the large black trunk with its key in the lock. A newly-lit taper stood on the candle holder in the center of the table like an eerie sentinel. There was a strong scent within, like lamp oil or kerosene. A desperate feeling overtook Lucy as she stood in the center of the room, the knife shaking in her hand.

"Harold ..." Lucy whimpered.

*"Lucy!"*

Lucy nearly shrieked at the sound of the voice which, seemed to be coming from the trunk.

"Harold!" she cried. "Where is she?"

"I don't know, just let me *out* of here!"

Lucy rushed toward the trunk and turned the key; an instant later Harold popped up like a Jack-in-the-Box. As they were starting toward the door, they heard the sound suddenly of wooden heels coming down the corridor.

"What should we do?" Lucy whispered feverishly.

"Quick! Back in the trunk!" Harold hissed.

They climbed in, and Harold brought the lid down just as the governess rounded the doorway. There was a long silence, then the sound of footsteps coming closer, and finally a low groan and creaking, like pulleys lowering a great weight. The key turned in the lock and was withdrawn, replaced by Caster's eye, staring in at them. The garret was suddenly filled with wild, piercing laughter. There was a small *tick*, followed by a *whoosh*, and then a series of rapid footfalls moving through the room and then down the hall, accompanied by more feral laughter.

Harold was shouting, slamming at the lid. Lucy began shouting too, for help, for the servants, for their parents, for anyone. But no one came. And as the flames rose around them, Harold and Lucy held each other and cried.

# THE BLACK BOOK OF NOTHINGS

We all live in the shadows of the dead. For some it's our fathers in their graves. For others it's our brothers, lost to the battlefield.

For me, it's the men and women for whom I fashion my wares. Author Wesley Holden lives in the shadow of his literary hero, a bygone pulp writer who met a mysterious end. When he finds a connection to his ~~idol~~ ~~idol~~ idol in an old notebook, Wesley risks turning the entire world into a graveyard.

# THE BLACK BOOK
# OF NOTHINGS

"They hate it!" Wes lamented into his phone. "Everyone hates it!" Tabitha sighed, her frustration transferred across satellites and continents to Wes's ear.

"That's not true, Wes. You know you overreact."

"Have you looked online? *The Times* called it a vapid example of paint by numbers fiction."

"Didn't I tell you not to read reviews anymore?"

"And *Weird Fiction Reader* says …"

"It doesn't matter what they said," Tabitha interrupted, "because you don't write weird fiction. You write supernatural thrillers and dark urban fantasy."

"It's all horror, Tabitha."

"Not to the algorithms and not to our bank accounts."

Wes glared at his computer monitor. The *Publisher's Weekly* review of his book taunted him. The light from the screen dared him to read the unkind words again and again.

*While Wesley Holden's language and pacing show that he is a writer of moderate skill, the derivative nature of his latest offering spotlights a startling lack of imagination that has become the hallmark of his work.*

"No one gives a shit about reviews. People are buying the book in droves," Tabitha insisted. "It's a New York Times Bestseller and you optioned the film rights before it even hit the shelves."

She had a point. Wes thought about the considerable advance he'd gotten for *Dead Body Blues* and for the two books before that, as well as the movie money that was coming in. The sudden wealth didn't completely heal his pride, but it lessened the sting of criticism.

"Go enjoy your success. You have enough money to do just about whatever you want. Buy a wildly impractical car. Get out of that shitty, little town and shack up with a hooker in Vegas for the week. Go do whatever you need to do to clear your mind for the next book."

"You're right, Tabitha," Wes said, though his line of thinking was much different than hers. He did have enough money to do whatever he wanted, but he didn't want to sleep with prostitutes or drive fast cars, or any such materialistic thing. He wanted to write an exceptional book. Not just a fun read, but something deeply evocative and entirely unmarketable.

Wes had enough money to last him the rest of his life and then some. He could afford to write bravely now. He didn't need to chase trends or worry about mass-market appeal. Who cared if his next book bombed or even if it killed his career? So long as it resonated with people in a lasting and meaningful way, that would be enough for him.

## 0

Wes walked down the abandoned train tracks that ran parallel to Aspen Street. The trees lining either side were still rich with green foliage, but the first bit of fall chill hung in the air. Sparse, yellowing grass dotted the ground between the ancient railroad ties and pale green weeds wrapped themselves around rusted iron rails.

The path along the old tracks was Wes' favorite place in Enfield. It was set back from the main road, away from the noise of morning traffic and the bustle of pedestrians heading out for their morning Starbucks. Few others ever wandered down the path, just the occasional mountain biker or dog walker.

Best of all, it was a dead zone—there was absolutely zero cell service. Tabitha couldn't hound him to churn out the next vacuous page-turner. His phone couldn't erupt with the Pavlovian dings and dongs of this or that notification. No phone calls. No email. No distractions. It was just him and his thoughts.

Wes wondered if the mediocrity of his writing could be blamed, at least in part, on the short digital leash that came with embracing modernity. Were these brief morning walks not enough time to properly cultivate the imagination? How could original thoughts foster when the mind is constantly barraged by corporate storytelling?

Wes thought of S. E. Lynch, his favorite author and the reason he'd moved to Enfield. He imagined Lynch walking down the same tracks, as he was known to do, and how unburdened his mind must have been. What a wonderful feeling that must be, Wes mused, to breathe in fresh air and think up beautifully ghastly thoughts without the expectations of commercial success hanging over you like the sword of Damocles.

Lynch's existence had been rife with other problems. Despite his incredible talent, Lynch was widely unrecognized during his lifetime and hashed out a meager existence writing deeply emotional tales of existential terror in the heyday of 1980's popcorn horror. His one commercial success, a novel entitled *The War of Time's End*, never brought him a dime, as it wasn't published until after his disappearance in 1989.

From the brutal murder of his mother to the atrocities he witnessed and inflicted upon others in Vietnam, to years of debilitating alcoholism, Lynch's troubled life was meticulously documented in his journals and letters. A lifetime of tragedy and poverty had undoubtedly fueled the man's exceptional writing. Wes, who never wanted for any comfort, almost envied those hardships, and he was certainly jealous over the creativity they inspired.

Looking down at the tracks, Wes spotted the impression of a boot heel in the dirt. It couldn't have been left by Lynch, but Wes pretended it was. He placed his heel into the imprint and imagined the ghost of Lynch superimposed over himself—their strides mirroring one another across time.

Wes took the tracks as far as he could before reaching Olde Town Square. He stopped at the Front Street Café to grab a Chi Tea Latte and shake off the cold. If he really wanted to be like S. E. Lynch he would have gone for an Irish Coffee, but Wes wasn't much of a drinker, and certainly didn't have it in him to booze it up so early in the morning.

He left the café and stepped back into the cool autumn air. He turned down Washington Avenue, a street packed tight with three-story buildings that formed a sort of wind tunnel, and his body stiffened at the chill. He gripped his tea with both hands, his cold digits greedy for the warmth that bled through the cardboard cup.

Wes had meant to follow Washington all the way down to the bank of the Swift River. There was an ancient bench there where he liked to sit and jot down ideas about story and character. It was too cold to deal with the wind on Washington Ave, however, and certainly too cold to write at the river's edge. Instead, he took a left onto Bateman, which was sheltered from the wind and was rather sunny at this time of the morning.

Storefronts lined either side of the street, offices and apartments above them. To the casual observer it looked like any other strip of small-town consumerism, but Bateman Road was full of history. Wes strolled past the yoga studio on the corner, which had once been a Dojo where Lynch taught Vietnamese martial arts until his binge-drinking became too much.

Across the street was a bar dating back to the revolutionary period.

There had been another pub there before, a British loyalist hangout called The Red Flagon. A group of vigilante patriots burned the place down, with the loyalists inside. When it was rebuilt, they dubbed it the Crimson Cup. Few today realized that the crossed glasses on the sign were not meant to be holding red wine, but the blood of traitors.

Wes passed by a few more buildings, some of no great relevance, and others party to more recent tragedies, like the abandoned record store on the corner. One of the kids who'd worked there shot up the high school with his friends the year before. Wes peeked through a break in the craft paper taped on the windows and tried to imagine that sinister young man from the papers working the counter. What had gone so wrong in his life to drive him to what he'd done?

Yes, the town was rich with tragic history. Tabitha had tried talking him into moving to New York or L. A., someplace he could schmooze and network, but neither city inspired him. Enfield was a good place to write horror—an inspiration for deep, atmospheric, soul-wrenching terror. He needed to tap into that.

A block away from the record shop, sat a squat brick building on the corner of Bateman and Essex. The faded white lettering painted over the crumbling masonry read *Mike's Army Navy,* but these days the building was home to *Swift River Consignment.* Plastic adhesive letters, the kind you might use on a mailbox, declared the name across the glass of the front door.

The windows on either side of the door were lined with eye-catching oddities and nostalgic trinkets. A collection of pinned butterflies was displayed beside a series of NES cartridges lined up like dominos. A black and white Furby stared out through the glass, a framed newspaper clipping from the Boston Molasses Flood behind it.

Wes considered the Molasses Flood for a moment. He'd read about the event before, a tragic accident where several people were trapped and cooked in burning hot molasses after a tank burst. Was there a kernel of a story there? Wes thought there might be.

He decided to see what other inspiration he might find inside the shop. A bell above the door chimed as he entered. A bored twenty-something looked up from the counter, grunted at him, then went back to staring at her phone.

The consignment shop had been on his list of places to check out since he'd moved to Enfield, but he'd never gotten around to it, until now. The place was a labyrinth of mismatched shelving—a mixture of stacked wooden cubbies, floor-to-ceiling bookshelves, and planks of raw lumber resting on rusty brackets.

Wes thumbed through milk crates full of worn magazines and old records. Finding nothing of interest, he moved further down the maze-like aisles of the store, past a wall of DVDs and VHS tapes and a curio cabinet filled with porcelain dolls. A Spinner rack of yellowed postcards, all filled out on the back but robbed of their stamps, sat beside a massive bookshelf. Beat up paperbacks, hardcovers with missing dust jackets, and weathered journals were packed, two deep in some places, with more volumes laying horizontally on top of them.

Wes started at the top shelf and looked at every book. Most of them were mass-market paperbacks, out of print and long forgotten. He frowned at this, thinking about how each represented a dream come true for some author, and how these brittle, uncared-for volumes represented the death of those dreams.

One book caught his attention, a worn black moleskin notebook, with no writing on the spine. Wes pulled the book from the shelf. The cover was plain as well, bearing no stamps or markings. He opened it to the first page and gasped.

*The Black Book of Nothings*
*By S. E. Lynch*

It was impossible. There was no way this book could have been sitting in a consignment shop all these years without someone realizing what it was, and yet... The words, all printed neatly and leaning to the left, were written a bit too large, as if by someone with failing vision.

Wes had read all of Lynch's letters and owned several of his original manuscripts. This was S. E. Lynch's handwriting. There was no doubt.

"The Black Book of Nothings," he whispered, his voice full of awe. This was Lynch's lost swan song. There had been references of it in a few of his letters to his former publisher, but no one had ever seen a manuscript. The few Lynch historians out there believed he'd come up with the title with no intention of writing it, just to scam his publisher out of an advance to feed his addictions, but here it was.

Giddy nervousness overtook Wes. He felt like he was about to cliff dive in some exotic paradise or kiss a girl for the first time all over again. Teary-eyed with excitement he turned the page, and his heart sank. A number of pages had been torn out, and the rest was blank.

Wes' shoulders fell and he let out a deep sigh. So, it was true, he thought, Lynch never even started the story. *The Black Book of Nothings* was true to its name.

*Still,* Wes thought to himself, *this proves he had at least intended to write it.* There was a value to the book, despite it being largely vacant of words. What Wes held in his hands may very well be the last thing S. E. Lynch ever tried to write. There was a certain breed of magic in that idea—the limitless potential of the blank pages, left vacant all these years, waiting for a pen to imbue them with life.

"This is what I will write," Wes whispered. "I'll pick up where Lynch left off."

The idea wasn't wholly original. A few other devotees of S. E. Lynch's work had borrowed the name for their own works of pastiche, but none of them were very good. They read like anemic imitations of the master, imitating the superficial elements of his work without offering any of the substance that was so rich in the original.

Wes' attempt would be different. He understood Lynch in a way that few others did. There was a spiritual kinship there—a bond that transcended death and time. And if that were not strong enough, then, of course, there was the journal in his hand—a direct physical link to Lynch.

The girl at the counter didn't seem to notice Wes' enormous grin or the nervous energy he was letting off. She chewed her gum, barely acknowledging him, and keyed the price of the book into the register. It came to three dollars even. Wes handed her a ten and told her to keep the change.

0

*Solomon stood on the River's Edge and stared at the cloven horizon. The jagged tear in the sky was monolithic, stretching up like a skyscraper in the middle of the Swift River. Utter blackness filled its dimensions—a purer black than any man had ever seen. It made the darkest night look gray by comparison.*

*It was not a black hole. Solomon had read about black holes before. The geometry of this thing was all wrong. It was not a neat, compressed orb, but an asymmetric spire. Furthermore, black holes were supermassive and endlessly supped upon the stuff of the universe, but this scar on the horizon gave as much as it took. In a grim process of cosmic respiration, it inhaled light and life and breathed onyx mist out over the river.*

*Those black wisps did not burn away like fog beneath the morning sun but floated across the river—dread spirits defiant of the dawn. Solomon watched those tendrils latch onto joggers like spectral lampreys and creep into the mouths of children taking the riverwalk to school. They all kept about their day as if nothing were wrong. Like the fissure on the horizon, only Solomon could see the alien mist.*

0

Wes smiled at the words in the notebook. It was only three paragraphs, which was a negligible amount for a writer who pumped out work as quickly as he did, but he knew they were the right words. He'd thrown away all the rules he'd had hammered into his head by professors, agents, and publishers. To hell with Hemmingway and Orwell and all the other advocates of clean, concise prose. The chains of "good taste" lay shattered at his feet. He'd embraced verbosity and the beautiful depth of language. Never had he felt so free.

Something in the back of his mind, that ceaseless ambition that drove him to success and chastised him for laziness, urged him to keep writing. Wes wasn't ready, however. He had the opening, but he wasn't sure where he wanted the story to go, and he wasn't going to rush this one.

With any other book, he'd break the story down into a formulaic structure. He had dozens of these he'd worked with as models for his other books. There was the hero's journey and Dan Harmon's story circle, both very reliable methods for crafting a story, as well as beat diagrams he'd made for his favorite comics, novels, and movies. *The Black Book of Nothings* demanded a more fluid approach than that. He knew in his bones that he couldn't drape this story upon a second-hand architecture.

Wes closed the book and stroked the leather cover. He'd come back to it later. For now, he needed the story to marinate in his mind. He needed to ponder and daydream and let his neurons conjure up monsters. For Wes, nothing was more conducive to courting creativity than fresh air and open space.

He packed the moleskin notebook into his messenger bag, put on a thin jacket, and left the house. The day had warmed up a bit and the sun shined bright in the cloudless sky. Upon making his way downtown, Wes turned onto Washington Avenue. The morning breeze had died and with it the wind tunnel effect that plagued that particular street.

Wes strolled past storefronts, offices, and restaurants paying no mind to any of them. His thoughts were with his story. Wild breeds of monsters and specters—potentialities of what may lie beyond the tear in the sky—populated his thoughts. Were they manifestations of sin and hate, pouring through a gate to hell? Could they be the revenants from some extinct world, seeking new flesh and a new home? Were they something born of his protagonist's mind—manifestations of grief and trauma made real?

Perhaps it didn't matter what was on the other side. He could keep things ambiguous and leave the reader to speculate and theorize. That's what he loved most about S. E. Lynch's work—the way that his tales raised far more questions than they ever answered.

Washington Ave ended at a T with Swift River Ave, a twisting road that followed the water. The walk signal was counting down numbers and a robotic voice repeated the word "walk" over and over. Wes approached the crosswalk then made his way to the opposite side of the street. He continued onto the grassy riverside beyond, where his favorite bench waited for him. There was something comforting about the weathered planks covered in crude graffiti and carved obscenities.

Wes retrieved the moleskin notebook from his bag, along with a blue gel pen. He tapped the capped pen against the open page and tried to figure out the details of his protagonist. Who was Solomon?

An angsty teenager? No, he didn't want to write about a kid. His agent would see it and try to make him turn the book into a YA novel or a King/McCammon coming-of-age novel.

A brainy introvert? No again. The world of horror didn't need another Lovecraftian intellectual.

His protagonist needed grit and attitude. He needed to be stern enough to face whatever alien horror was seeping into the world, but also a touch mad—part Lemmy Kilmister with a touch of Colonel Walter Kurtz.

A clear vision of the character came into Wes' mind—a rugged, middle-aged man in a ratty, olive-drab jacket and yellow tobacco stains in his fu Manchu mustache. Wes could envision the brittle, split ends of the character's ponytail and his dry, cracked knuckles. He could see the haunted look in his green, tired eyes. It was the spitting image of S. E. Lynch.

"Solomon." Wes laughed. "Solomon Edward Lynch." *The Black*

*Book of Nothings* was going to be Lynch's swan song, so Wes supposed it made sense to pay homage to the man himself.

Wes wrote like a madman. His pen moved furiously across the page, and he expanded the opening chapter by several pages while cramming the margins full of shorthand notes.

The critics had always panned his originality, and he believed they were right to, but Wes was excellent at the nuts and bolts of writing. He wove in details about his protagonist with each new paragraph and brought the character of Solomon to life in a slow, organic manner, never info-dumping or getting bogged down in exposition.

He finished the first scene and capped it with a triple cross, the way he always did when writing longhand. His lips curled into a smile as he read over that first scene. It was unlike any work he'd ever produced, and he loved it.

Wes closed the book, leaned back, and stared out over the river. He imagined the torn horizon from his story—that black, jagged scar across the sky. What would it be like to see something like that—something so terrible and surreal—and to have it be invisible to everyone else?

A shiver went through Wes' body, and he suddenly felt that inextricable buzz in his head that one gets when they're being watched. He shifted on the bench to look behind him and nearly yelped.

A grizzled man in a threadbare olive drab jacket stood several feet behind him. A cigar hung from his chapped lips, below his yellowed mustache. His green eyes were locked on the horizon, his expression a mix of tired anguish and obstinate resentment.

"Solomon?"

The man didn't answer.

Wes followed the man's gaze to the skyline over the river. There was nothing there to be fixated on—no boats, or birds, or floating trash— just the blue sky and the neighboring town of Prescott across the water.

When Wes turned back around, the man was gone.

0

*Ronald K. Levi sipped his coffee and watched the world pass by through the plate glass window of his favorite café. An advance copy of a mass-market science fiction novel sat on the table beside his notebook. There were post-it notes, scrawled with shorthand marking pages and passages of interest— overly descriptive sections that dragged down the story, irredeemable characters that romanticize anti-social behavior, and moments of deus ex-machina.*

*In all honesty, it was an entertaining book, but it wasn't art. It didn't have the timely messages or the masterful prose of* White Noise *or* The Handmaid's Tale. *Sure, it was fun, but his readers didn't want to hear that.*

*People read his reviews for two reasons. The first was so that they could steal his talking points on more highbrow literature, and speak about the books as if they had read or cared about them. The second reason was to take pleasure in his meanness toward any book that didn't meet his stringent ideas of what qualifies as art. He often mixed in* ad hominem *insults against the author in such reviews, and readers seemed to eat that up.*

*Ronald felt the hairs on the back of his neck stand on end. He cringed and shrugged his shoulders as a chill shot through his body. Turning, he saw nothing behind him that might cause such a sensation. No one was glaring at him, and everything seemed normal in the café. College students sat with their noses in textbooks and a pair of cops ate pastries at the counter.*

*When he turned around, Ronald found a man sitting across from him. He let out a gasp and jumped up in his seat. His knee hit the table, causing a bit of coffee to splash out of his cup and onto his notebook.*

*The man across from him was dressed in a dirty, ragged jacket that looked like it came from an Army surplus store. His long, ratty hair was tied back, and days of stubble framed an uneven fu Manchu mustache. A cloud of putrid aromas hung over him—cigar smoke and cheap booze. Ronald figured him a vagrant.*

*"Sorry, pal, this table's taken."*

*The man picked up the sci-fi novel from the table and started flipping through the pages, looking at each of Ronald's handwritten post-its as he did. He read each one aloud as he came to them.*

*"Altruistic, responsible characters painted as boorish drones." The man tore the note from the book, crumpled it, and tossed it to the floor.*

*"Superficial. Lacking statement and meaning," he said, dropping the paper into the spilled coffee.*

*"The spelling bee vocabulary of the story comes across as pretentious and ostracizes readers from both deeply rural and urban areas." The man held this one up and shook his head slowly.*

*"So, you're saying poor folks are too dumb to appreciate the book? Such a progressive insight."*

*Ronald went to speak, but the crazy man cut him off with a hissing shush.*

*"How much time do you think ..." the man looked at the cover of the paperback and read the author's name. "...Jackson R. Curtis spent writing this? How many early mornings and late nights do you think go into crafting nebulous musings into a hundred-thousand-word narrative?*

*"Tell me something, Ronald. Have you ever created anything in your life? Have you ever known what it's like to draw threads of naught through the veil of worlds that is the mind, and weave them into something that can be loved and shared? Or have you always simply shit on those who do?"*

*"Do I know you?" Ronald stammered.*

*"In a sense," The man said, lighting up a cigarette. "You know my words. You gave them the same hatchet job you're planning to deliver to Mr. Curtis here."*

*Ronald looked back at the cops sitting at the counter. He swallowed hard and considered calling for them, but the vagrant laughed. It was a cold and mirthless sound.*

*"Don't bother. People like me—the broken vets, the addicts and the drunks—we're the world's refuse. Who wants to hold onto a broken tin*

*soldier? They just pretend we don't exist, and I've found little bits of magic to help them do so more efficiently."*

*"Who are you?" Ronald swallowed hard. "What do you want?"*

*"The name's Solomon, and you once wrote that if I had a muse, it was a dead prostitute. I guess that's your poetic way of saying my work was cheap and lifeless, with a veneer of pretty words, Maybe you were right, but I want to introduce you to my new muse. She's far more giving but demands much more."*

*Ronald couldn't see the jagged slit in space and time that marred the air behind Solomon. His terrestrial vision did not allow him to view the terrible and formless things seeping out of that fissure. He could, however, feel the frigid touch of the unthing which crawled into his lungs and took his body for its own. It felt like he'd breathed in ice water, and he trembled helplessly as his consciousness was devoured.*

◊

The phone rang, waking Wes from a nightmare of being held like livestock in a bamboo cage where incorporeal monsters formed from the shadows of trees and the smoke from artillery. The weird, inconsistent narrative of the dream was already fading as he fumbled for his cell phone. By the time he sat up all that was left were non sequitur images—poems written in blood across flat stones, dead-eyed GIs with gaping head wounds, and swarms of hungry insects.

"Hello." Wes rubbed his tired eyes, only to find that his face was wet with tears. The dream had been so intense, that he'd been crying in his sleep.

"Good afternoon, Sunshine," Tabitha said, her voice ringing with practiced optimism. "Are you just waking up?"

"Um … yeah," Wes grumbled. "What time is it?"

"Almost noon, assuming you haven't taken my advice and gone on vacation in a different time zone."

"No, I'm still in Enfield. I guess I was just up too late writing."

"That's what I like to hear!" Tabitha exclaimed. "So, you've started the new book? How's it coming? What's it about?"

"I don't want to talk about it until it's done. I'd rather you read it cold. It's coming along though. I think I've got something special here—something pricks like Ronald Levi won't be able to say boo about."

"Well, I umm … I wouldn't worry about Ronald Levi saying much of anything. He died early this morning. It's all over my Facebook page."

Wes didn't respond—he couldn't respond. His chest tightened and his breath came in gasps.

"You alright, Wes? I didn't think you'd be too broken up about Ronald of all people, especially after that last review."

Wes grabbed the moleskin notebook from his nightstand and opened the page marked by its ribbon. He reread the last scene that he'd written—a scene written solely for catharsis and not intended for the final draft. Ronald's name stood out like an accusing spirit.

"How?" Wes gasped, trying to compose himself. "How did he die?"

"Not sure. Word is he was out for his morning coffee and went into a seizure of some sort. A friend of a friend's boyfriend said it was an ugly scene. Poor guy was stiff and blue in the face before the ambulance could break through the rush hour traffic."

Wes looked down at the page. There it was—a terrible prophecy written in his own hand.

*… the frigid touch of the unthing … crawled into his lungs.*

It was a coincidence. It had to be. Still, Wes thought of how he'd spotted the late Solomon Edward Lynch gazing over the Swift River … just where he'd placed him in the story. That had come true, and now this had as well.

◊

*Solomon sat on a stool, in a bar full of corpses—dead men and women with faces blackened by frostbite. A TV over the bar showed scenes of devastation in Boston and New York. Trembling lunatics with pale blue complexions and crumbling golems—animated idols and fossils come to life—clashed with cops and National Guardsmen who all looked pallid with sickness. The green patina of Lady Liberty had turned black and brown, and that icon of freedom lay like a fetid corpse on the bank of the Hudson.*

*Solomon used the clicker to flip from one news station to the next, surveying the devastation. The nightmare had spread to the rest of the world, as well. America couldn't hold it any more than Enfield could. Whatever had been birthed over the Swift River had now poisoned the entire globe.*

*He took a swig of whiskey from the bottle, not the rotgut crap that was the staple of his diet, but the top-shelf stuff. Never being particularly good with money, Solomon rarely had a chance to drink good booze, but the upside of the apocalypse was that it came with an open bar.*

*The door to the bar opened and the bell over the threshold rang out. Solomon kept drinking and watching the TV. He didn't need to turn around. He knew who was there.*

0

Wes walked through the ghost town of Enfield. He'd been writing non-stop for days, or maybe weeks, and he couldn't remember the last time he'd slept, never mind left the house. The devastation did not surprise him, however, despite how deeply the town had fallen into ruin. He'd seen it all in his mind from the decaying offal of human remains to the stumbling living statues of virgin mothers and plastic, pop culture simulacra, to the vaporous monsters that darkened the heavens like storm clouds.

Most of the world hadn't seen the dark forces that brought disaster with them through the rift, but Wes now did. In writing *The Black Book of Nothings*—in visualizing the terrors and articulating their form—he had developed eyes to see. He'd glimpsed the black gate over the Swift River and he presently watched the vaporous monstrosities from the other side slither beneath doors and float through open windows. Enfield had been transformed into a graveyard and there were few living beings for them to find, but those things never stopped hunting. They burned through hosts so quickly—Terran matter was simply too fragile to contain them.

He wasn't sure why they never bothered with him. Maybe they saw him as a father or even as a god—the terrible mind that had conjured them into being. It didn't matter. Not everything had to be spelled out. It was okay to be ambiguous. That's why he'd loved Solomon Lynch, and why he'd written this story with that same nebulous approach.

Wes walked up to the door of *The Crimson Cup*. It was the only building with the lights on, and he could hear the exhausted drone of a traumatized newscaster through the door. The air inside wreaked of death and waste, smoke and booze.

Solomon Edward Lynch sat at the bar, just where Wes had written him. The grizzled author raised a bottle of whiskey to the sky in a silent salute.

"Solomon?"

Solomon Lynch turned toward Wes, a cigar clamped between his teeth. He nodded, a knowing expression on his face. His manner was cool and unworried, despite the world crumbling around them.

"Come have a seat, youngblood."

Wes sat down beside his literary idol—a man who was supposed to be thirty years in the grave, yet sat drinking whiskey before his eyes. Solomon offered the bottle to Wes. He took a swallow and watched the end of the world unfold on the television.

"How did this happen?" Wes Asked.

"The same way most things do, I reckon. A musing is snatched from the ethereal, beaten into shape by the force of imagination, and birthed into being by the divine spark of the human will.

"Ever hear of Austin Osman Spare? He was an occultist who believed he could transform his intent into a sigil, then charge it with his will to actualize it. In Chaos traditions the magician concentrates on a singular focus, eschewing all other thoughts, in order to manifest his desire. It's the same thing we writers do, at least the best among us. Instead of sigils or rituals, we use narrative and prose. Stories are our singular focus. It's no surprise that our dreams occasionally come true."

Solomon savored a drag of his cigar, then blew the smoke into the air. He sat in silence for a moment, admiring the burning tip of his cigar.

"Or maybe it's a cursed notebook or some other hackneyed bullshit," Solomon added. "What the hell do I know?"

The image on the television turned sidewise, then the screen went black. Solomon changed the channel, clicking through several stations before finding anything. Wes wondered how long it would be until the last broadcast ceased.

"I didn't mean for things to go this far,"

"You could have stopped, "Solomon said, "Could have put the pen down and walked away."

"No, I don't think I could have."

"Then it sounds like you're the real deal, young blood—a slave to the page. My condolences."

"What did you do? How did you stop it when you tried to write it?"

Solomon took a long drag from his cigar, then placed the tip against a napkin. He let it burn on the bar and gazed into the flames.

"It doesn't matter what I did or what I wrote. This is your story now, kid. So, you tell me, how does it end?"

Wes took another swig of whiskey and opened the *Black Book of Nothings*. The paper seemed to vibrate beneath his fingers. He placed his pen against the page. Oceans boiled at turns of a phrase. Sentences toppled mountains and brought the Earth to a cosmic standstill. No matter where the unthings tried to live—no matter what they possessed, they were anathema to the physical universe and no comfort could be found there.

Stymied by the entropy of existence, and urged on by Wes' pen, the vaporous monsters fled whence they came, dragging along he who had summoned them into the gaping wound on the horizon. When Wes penned the words *the end,* it really was, for him at least.

◊

*Weird Fiction Reader* review of *The Black Book of Nothings* By Wesley Holden

Wesley Holden is a complicated author. There is no denying that he can turn a phrase with the best and that he holds the ability to arouse the imagination of the masses. His clean, conversational style, both pedestrian and compulsively readable, has allowed him to enjoy a massive fanbase and immense commercial success.

On the other hand, his work is highly derivative, often watering down the themes of greater talents and reducing thoughtful metaphor to cheap window dressing. Starting with his breakout novel, *Chernobyl House*, a low-brow modernization of William Hope Hodgson's *The House on the Borderland*, Holden has displayed a talent for repackaging the ideas of bygone masters to meet the commercial yearnings of the contemporary zeitgeist.

Holden has been the subject of harsh criticism due to his lack of imagination, sometimes unduly. I personally must admit that I have been overly critical of his work in the past, perhaps because I've seen him outshine so many of his more talented peers. Recognizing this, I tried my best to go into *The Black Book of Nothings* with as open a mind as possible.

I have read this novel three times over, and I still don't know quite what to make of it. It is apparent from the first paragraph that we are dealing with a different Wesley Holden. The straightforward writing of his previous work is abandoned in lieu of a style that is both lyrical and visually evocative. The writing maintains a sense of modern accessibility while drawing upon the strength of poetic fantasists like Lord Dunsany and S. E. Lynch. While Hemmingway might turn in his grave at Holden's betrayal of invisible prose, I see it as a welcome growth.

The plot is where things start to break down for me, and all the beautiful words in the world can't save a bad story. The Black Book of Nothings starts well enough, with a haggard man named Solomon gazing at a terror that none but him can see. We soon learn that the protagonist is a fictionalized version of author S. E. Lynch, who reemerged after his disappearance decades before.

This odd choice of protagonist stinks of pastiche and fanfic and makes the admirable change in Holden's style less impactful. Maybe I could have gotten past all this, if not for the cyclone of self-indulgence that follows. The central mysteries of the book and the apocalyptic horrors that fill it take a back seat to a barrage of wish fulfillment, personal attacks against critics, and ham-fisted meta-fiction.

Perhaps the greatest Blunder is made at the climax, where Holden robs the fictional version of S. E. Lynch of all agency and inserts himself as the crux of the story, the hidden protagonist, and ultimately the hero as he sacrifices his own existence to the pages of the titular notebook in order to contain an ill-defined apocalypse.

In all honesty, I don't think this book would have ever been published if not for Holden's inexplicable disappearance upon finishing the manuscript. Maybe that's why Holden took off—to force the publisher's hand. I hope it's something like that and not a more dire situation. Despite my harsh words about his work, Holden is an author of adequate talent and I pray for his safety.

Assuming he is alive and well and continues writing, I can see The Black Book of Nothings marking an awkward but important step toward a more mature Wesley Holden—one that could live up to all the hype and bridge the gap between mass-market horror and thoughtful weird fiction.

# THE NEGATIVE

There! Polished to a mirror shine!
I can almost see myself in it — well, not in that way.
This story features mirrors too. There are also some
teenagers, an encyclopedia of the supernatural, a
very angry girl, an entity summoned in a looking
glass during an innocent game.

But is the thing pursuing Melinda a malevolent
being, or a reflection of herself?

# THE NEGATIVE

"What do you guys want to do now?" Melinda asked. Her birthday had been a non-stop flow of shopping and eating and talking. Now, back in her bedroom with her three closest friends and the detritus of a day at the mall surrounding them (plastic bags, plastic hangers, plastic packaging), the conversation had finally ebbed, and there had been silence for the last five minutes during which Alicia texted, Stephanie flipped through a new book, and Jessica bit her nails while Melinda painted her own an obnoxious shade of neon green with a glittery clear-coat finish.

"Anybody feel like watching a movie? I just downloaded this great art documentary," Melinda offered.

"Nah," said Jessica, sucking a bleeding cuticle.

Alicia tapped her phone and began to giggle. She showed it to Jessica, who snickered, then turned it toward Melinda. On the screen was a picture of an underwear model bulging his boxer briefs.

"Hey Mel, is *this* what Tyson looked like?"

"I bet that'll be your b-day present from him. Probably with a bow tied around it," said Jessica.

"Leave her alone you guys," Stephanie said. Melinda smiled. She could always count on Steph.

"Whatever. You can believe she's a virgin but she's not fooling me," said Alicia.

"All I did was *touch* it," Melinda said angrily. Jessica and Alicia erupted into hysterics. Downstairs, Melinda heard her father mutter something, followed by an increase in the TV volume. "*Shhhh, you guys! My dad's going to freak out!*" she hissed.

Stephanie looked up from her book. "You guys want to call a ghost?"

"*That's* what you're reading about?" said Jessica. "I thought it was a cookbook or something."

"It's a collection of spells," said Stephanie. She showed them the cover. There was a smoking black cauldron, a rack of phials filled with red liquid of various shades, and a pair of severed bird feet beside a pile of finely-ground purple powder on a wooden chopping block. "This one's for summoning the dead. You say their name in the mirror fifty times and—"

"And they're supposed to appear," Alicia finished.

"Yeah, *everybody's* done that, Steph," said Jessica.

"*Bloody Mary, Bloody Mary,*" said Alicia mockingly.

"No, it's not like that," said Stephanie.

"Sounds like it to me," said Jessica.

"I think it sounds fun," said Melinda. "Jess, can we borrow your compact?"

"You know I don't carry that kind of shit. Ask the cheerleader," said Jessica. Alicia, half listening, half focusing on something on the phone screen, frowned in an oddly detached way without looking up.

"That won't work anyway. It has to be a bathroom mirror," said Stephanie.

"Why?" said Melinda.

"Because it's ..." she paused, locating the quote on the page. "...'the place where we see ourselves most honestly.'"

"What do you guys think? Want to try it?" said Melinda, already rising.

A non-committal moan came from Jessica and Alicia, but Stephanie said yes, and followed Melinda into the hall with the others reluctantly in tow. They passed through Melinda's father's room, which was dark and smelled vaguely of pine scented cologne, and entered the bathroom. The moonlight coming through the privacy glass cast a mottled shadow on the wall. There were four large panel mirrors above the double sink. Alicia immediately planted herself on the toilet lid, her face illuminated by smartphone light, while Stephanie centered herself in front of the mirrors with Melinda next to her. Jessica, standing with her thumbs in her belt loops, reached out and flipped on the light.

"No, it has to be dark!" said Stephanie, hitting the switch. "Now, we have to think of someone dead. Alicia, will you shut that thing off?" The latter complied with a huff.

"Michael Jackson," Jessica said.

Alicia laughed. Even Melinda smiled.

"It can't be someone famous," said Stephanie.

"Why not?" said Jessica.

"Because famous people never show up."

"He's probably busy getting another nose job anyway, wherever he is."

"We could try my Uncle Cornbread," said Jessica.

"*Uncle Cornbread?*" said Alicia.

"Yeah, he was my dad's brother. He got hit by a train before I was born."

"Why'd they call him that?" said Melinda.

"He had like, yellow teeth or something."

"Gross, Jess," said Stephanie.

"How about Jimmy Acton," said Melinda.

"Who?" said Stephanie.

"That kid who died of spinal meningitis when we were in second grade," said Alicia.

The four looked at each other and shrugged. Jessica volunteered. She pushed between Stephanie and Melinda, stared straight into the mirror at her own pudgy, makeup-less face, lifted her hands like a priest at communion and said: "I call James Acton."

"No, not like that," said Stephanie. "You have to say it fifty times, remember?"

Jessica scoffed, looked back into the mirror and said 'James Acton' fifty times. Nothing happened. "It didn't work."

"It's because you said 'James' instead of 'Jimmy'," said Melinda.

"Let me try one," said Alicia.

"Who?" said Stephanie.

"Mr. Janek."

"Why, because you had a crush on him in junior high?" said Jessica.

"I did not!"

"It's not funny you guys. My grandma died of cancer too. I feel bad for his wife. They'd just had a baby," said Melinda.

"Let's call your grandma, Mel!" said Jessica.

"Really Jess? My *grandma*?"

Jessica looked down at the floor and muttered a *sotto voce* apology.

"Let's try Mr. Janek," said Stephanie. Alicia looked into the mirror and said 'Todd Janek' fifty times while absently toying with her hair. Again, nothing.

"This is stupid. It doesn't work," said Jessica.

"I don't know any more dead people you guys!" said Alicia.

"The book says that if you have trouble reaching a specific spirit, you can try calling a random ghost," said Stephanie.

"You should try it, birthday girl," said Jessica, punching Melinda in the arm. Melinda winced. Downstairs, she heard the TV turn off and her father shuffling into the kitchen. He would be coming up to bed as soon as he set the coffee pot for the morning.

"Fine. I'll try it. What am I supposed to say, 'random ghost?'"

"Say 'any ghost,'" Stephanie said.

Melinda stared at herself in the mirror. Her eyes looked like pools of oil and her hair two black brushstrokes on either side of her pale face.

"Any ghost. Any ghost. Any ghost. Any ghost. Any ghost …" she said. "Any ghost any ghost any ghost any ghost any ghost any ghost any ghost any ghost any ghost any ghost …"

After twenty-five times, it all began to run together.

"Anyghostanyghostanyghostanyghostanyghostanyghostanyghos tanyghostanyghostanyghostanyghostanyghostanyghostanyghosta nyghost …"

Around forty, the two words stopped being words and became a single sound, like a birdcall—

"…eneekoseneekoseneekosainegoseainegoseainegosenegoasenegoa senegoasenegoas …"

At fifty, she heard a sound like fingertips rubbing together in her ears. The other girls were fading, the room became winter-cold and all Melinda could see was her own blanched face glowing like the Worm Moon over a deep and dark forest. Thin fissures appeared along her forehead and spread rapidly down her cheeks. These lines softened, blotted like ink dripped onto paper, and soon her entire face was burn-black. It began to change, swell; her eyes became lightning-bright and her white lips spread into a huge smile, ragged as a hole punched through glass.

Then the light flipped on, and she was looking at herself again. The other girls were calling her name, shaking her, but Melinda couldn't answer. The face was still imprinted on her eyes, like an image burned there by the sun. She began to shudder, then hyperventilate.

"Mel. *Mel!*" Jessica kept repeating.

"Should we go get her dad?" Alicia said.

"Help me get her back to her room," said Stephanie. Melinda felt them un-sticking her fingers from the edge of the counter where they held as if super-glued. They ran into her dad in the hall. He was quite drunk and didn't acknowledge them at first. Then he saw his daughter and cocked his head concernedly.

"Everything all right, ladies?"

"Girl problems," said Jessica.

He frowned, then gave a little nod of comprehension and kissed Melinda on the forehead.

"Happy birthday, sweetheart. No drinking in there, girls," he said. A cloud of beer smell followed him down the hall to his bedroom.

Melinda was put on her bed, a blanket lain over her shoulders. After a couple silent minutes, Jessica turned to Alicia and said: "It's getting late. You want to get going?" Alicia, looking spooked, stood abruptly, said goodbye, and followed Jessica out the door. Melinda watched them leave, feeling embarrassed and angry despite her terror.

"Don't worry, I'm not going anywhere," said Stephanie. There was another long silence, but eventually the two began chatting casually; Melinda cocooned in her blanket, Stephanie straightening her hair in Melinda's vanity mirror. Reflected in the latter, hanging on the wall above a drawing table covered with paint tubes, brushes, pens and pencils, and a mortar and pestle was the painting which had won Melinda first prize for "mastery of perspective" in that year's school art competition. It was of a medieval castle in springtime. Yellow pennants flew from its twin turrets and revelers spilled out of its mouth over a stone bridge and up a tree-flanked path in the foreground. Fat ripe fruit hung from the trees, which the party plucked and passed to one another. Looking at the scene calmed her somewhat.

During a pause in the chit-chat, Stephanie looked at Melinda in the mirror and said: "You saw something, didn't you?"

Melinda nodded.

Stephanie completed a pass with the straightener and paused. A little wisp of steam rose off her hair. "What did it look like?"

"I don't want to talk about it right now," Melinda said.

Stephanie put down the hair tool, sat next to Melinda on the bed and put an arm around her. "Maybe tomorrow?"

"Maybe," Melinda said with a sniffle.

After Stephanie left, Melinda got into her pajamas and shut the light off. Before getting into bed, she took a black throw blanket from her closet and threw it over the vanity.

〇

"Do you know what happened to the bathroom mirror?"

Melinda was sitting at the kitchen table before a half-eaten bowl of soggy cereal and reading the same line over and over again in *Macbeth* when her father came downstairs, looking not so happy.

"What do you mean?"

"It's shattered. I know you girls were in there. I saw you, remember?" After seeing all the beer cans in the trash this morning, Melinda was surprised that *he* could remember.

"We didn't do it, dad."

"Who did then?"

Melinda didn't answer.

"Look, you're fifteen now. Fifteen-year-olds don't break things like little kids and leave them for adults to find."

"Dad, I *swear* I didn't!"

"Then it was one of your friends."

"You were in there after us! Wouldn't you have seen it if we had?"

His face went red. He closed his eyes, which were darkly ringed and puffy. When he spoke again, what came out was not what she expected.

"Are you still mad at your mother for not calling yesterday?"

"You know I don't care about that."

Her father dragged his fingers across his forehead. "Someone broke the mirror. It wasn't *me*, and if it wasn't *you*, then it was one of your friends." He picked up his briefcase and turned toward the front door. "So, here's the deal. Next time the girls come over, tell them to leave the booze at home or I'm calling their parents." And then he was out the door, slamming it before she could respond. Melinda watched through the rain-speckled bay window as his black sedan pulled out of the garage and sped off.

Melinda sat numbly at the table a moment. *It had to have been him*, she thought. She'd seen him weaving drunkenly at the sink a hundred times while doing the dishes, and now she pictured him leaning into the mirror to steady himself. He'd been downing a case of Old Steed tallboys a night since her mother left; this morning she'd even noticed a few whisky nips sprinkled between the crushed beer cans. He probably didn't remember.

Melinda's eyes drifted from her book to the shallow flight of stairs, and she thought *next time just push him. He'd be better off and you know it. Wonder if it's high enough?* She frowned, shaking off the uncharacteristically violent thought, then dog-eared her place in *Macbeth*, dumped her mushy cereal down the garbage disposal and went upstairs to have a look at the mirror.

His room smelled bad. The shades were drawn but some of the rainy daylight had managed to penetrate, giving the room a hazy appearance, as if someone had just finished smoking a cigarette. His bed stood against the far wall and his dresser was to the right of the door. Atop it was a bottle of that noxious pine cologne he invariably wore; a glass jar half-filled with coins; a few crumpled receipts; and a pile of dirty shirts. A wrinkled pant leg hung down over an open drawer. Her mother's white dresser stood across the room, blank and austere as a marble sarcophagus. Melinda went to it, recalling the things that used to be there: the antique jewelry box, the ceramic religious baubles, the silver tray lined with rows of perfume she rarely wore. The faint scent of them still lingered around it like a fading memory. She ran a finger across the dusty surface, thinking of her mother in the big southern city where she'd moved with her new boyfriend, and pictured all of those things arranged on some new dresser. It made Melinda sad, but it also pissed her off.

From where she now stood, she could see broken glass on the bathroom floor. Frowning, Melinda turned the corner and flipped on the light. Glass was everywhere—the counter, in the sink, on the bathmat, even atop the toilet. All the panels had some damage, but the third—the one where she'd seen the face—was the most catastrophic of the four. Long stalagmites and stalactites of mirror ran up and down from a plate-sized hole at its center. The break was odd; not the usual spiderweb pattern, but an explosion, as if something had come *through* rather than impacted it. As Melinda stared at her fractured reflection, she began to hear a sound: a palpable tremor in her brain—a grinding noise like a knife sharpening on a whetstone. Something began to rise above it, a stuttering laugh, an electronic bleating, cutting through the static.

Outside Tyson's truck rumbled into the driveway—sputtered, popped, and whinnied as he restarted it. A few seconds later he beeped the horn, silencing the static. Melinda blinked. The horn blared again, once short, then once long.

Melinda backed out of the room. She got her bag and book and headed for the front door, tracking bits of mirror glass as she walked.

0

Tyson held two to-go cups of coffee. He handed her one, shook his blonde hair out of his eyes with a single jerk of the head and kissed her. "How was your birthday?" he asked, looking over his shoulder as he backed out of the driveway.

Melinda took a drink of the coffee, which scorched the roof of her mouth despite careful sipping. "It was all right."

"Did you hang with Alicia by chance?"

"Yeah, why?"

"Cause she called me like five times."

"She did?"

"Mmm hmm," said Tyson. He took a couple big gulps from his cup and hit the scan button on the radio.

"Why would she do that?"

"I don't know. I thought you guys were pranking me, so I didn't answer. Probably just pocket dialing."

She eyed him suspiciously. "Has she called you before?"

"Well, you know, months ago. Before you and I started going out. But it was nothing."

He'd said it in a proud sort of way that bothered her. The scan function stopped on a station that was all static. Angrily she reached down to flip it off and noticed the numbers on the digital display screen were backwards. "What's wrong with your radio?"

Tyson looked down at it and raised an eyebrow. "Wrong with it?"

Melinda looked again and saw the numbers were normal again. The static rushed through her mind, fast and hissing like a passing car. She closed her eyes, drew in a sharp breath.

"Mel? You ok?"

"I don't know. I don't feel right."

"Was your dad being a dick again?"

"Kind of," she said. She set the coffee in a cup holder, crossed her arms over her chest and laid her head against the window, listening to the engine hum like a hive of bees.

0

During first period, Melinda's English teacher gave a computer presentation on *Macbeth*, but the text on the screen kept changing like the clock in Tyson's truck. The film in World History in the following class was no better; not only was it in French, but the subtitles were backwards.

She had a migraine by the end and vomited in the bathroom between classes. While rinsing her mouth in the sink, she heard something in the open stall behind her: breathing, moaning. Melinda shifted slightly to look behind her own reflection. Tyson was standing in the stall with his pants halfway down, Alicia in front of him. He turned and grinned—a grin that spread until his face was torn by it. Alicia looked around him, her long spindly fingers gripping the backs of his legs. Her eyes were holographic, her mouth like a bruise. She began to laugh; the sound was sandpaper on metal. Melinda screamed as she spun around.

The stall was empty.

Another girl came into the bathroom. She glanced at Melinda, then went into the stall, closed the door and latched it.

◊

Stephanie was a library aid during her free period. Melinda found her in the reference section, returning a cart full of books to the shelves. Melinda told her about what she'd seen the night earlier; about the broken mirror in her dad's bathroom; about the episode a few minutes earlier.

"I have this book … an encyclopedia of the supernatural," Stephanie said, "I'll bring it with me tomorrow. Meet me here in the morning before first period."

"What if I see it again? What should I do?"

"We'll figure it out. Call me if you're freaked out."

After school, Melinda took the bus instead of riding with Tyson. It wasn't what she'd seen Alicia doing to him in the mirror. She just couldn't think of his face now without that stretched smile.

◊

There was a contractor's truck in the driveway when she got home. Inside, Melinda found her father talking to a pair of guys in paint-spattered jeans. One of the men handed her father an estimate written on a flimsy sheet of yellow paper. He took it, glanced at it, then glared at Melinda.

57

She went upstairs, opened the door to her room and stared at the covered mirror for a few moments as if it were an animal about to strike. She jumped when her phone chimed. She took it out of her pocket and unlocked the screen. A text from Tyson—like everything else that day, the letters were backwards or upside down. She smacked it, turned the device off then on again—no change—though she was able to decode the message:

"Waited for u after school. Everything ok? How'd u get home?"

She typed: "Took the bus", paused, then added "Bad cramps. Sorry didnt text. Going to sleep. See u in morning <3"

Then she turned off the phone, tossed it on the night table and got in bed, pulling the blanket over her head. At length, she slept, but the static followed her under, into her half dreams—a sound that shouldn't be a sound, like worms moving through soil, like audible bit rot.

0

Melinda woke in the dark to voices in her room.

"I don't know. I haven't talked to her."

"Why don't you invite her down?"

A pause. "She's better off there, with her father. Those two are more alike than they realize."

"But don't you want to see her? She's your *daughter*, Jan."

"I just need a break right now. From *all* of it—including Melinda. It's bad enough I have her father leaving those pitiful messages every day."

Melinda opened her eyes. She could see light glowing through the blanket hanging over the vanity mirror. Slowly, she slid out of bed and approached it. The voices were muffled, like music playing in a passing car. She took a corner of the blanket and lifted it back. Sharp light—bright sun and blue sky—pierced her night eyes. Melinda put her hand up, wincing from the intensity of it. At length, once her vision had adjusted, she looked again, and saw her mother and a man sitting on a beach, their bodies brown and oily. The sea swelled and dipped behind them while seagulls pecked at a bloated fish in the background.

"I haven't told anyone this, but Sam wasn't the only reason I left. I never wanted to be a mother. It was *Sam* who wanted kids. You know, I almost lost her twice during the pregnancy. My life would have been … different, you know? And then we bring her home, and guess what? He doesn't want anything to do with her either. So here I am, twenty-one, with a baby *I* didn't ask for and a husband who can't or won't fuck me because he spends all his time with his lips on a bottle instead of—"

*You bitch. You lying, cheating bitch.* Melinda wanted to reach through the mirror, grab her mother by her dye-fried blond hair; wanted to feel it tearing from the scalp like a handful of grass from the ground. Yes—and now the other hand on her throat, the soft parts in there crunching, grating as Melinda squeezed. And it felt *good*—goddamn— not only the sensation, but the feeling of obeying an intuition which she hadn't realized was there always, requiring satisfaction. Her mother was looking at her now, her sunbaked body bog-mummy black. Her eyes were holographic, blinding as they caught the sunlight. A cloud of death gas poured from her gaping mouth as she laughed.

Melinda screamed, let the blanket fall back over the mirror and the room went instantly black again. A moment later she heard her father at the door, his voice sleepy and irritable. Just a nightmare, she told him. When she heard him walk off again, Melinda turned back toward the vanity mirror, covered with the black throw like a mourning looking glass, and decided she couldn't sleep in the same room with it. She went downstairs, laid on the couch, turned the TV on. She watched backwards infomercials for a couple hours until the windows began to gray, and it was time to get ready for school.

0

She found Stephanie at a table in the furthest corner of the library surrounded by walls of school year books and local histories. The book in front of Stephanie was large and old, with a white worn cover, fraying edges, and a dry and tattered binding. Embossed on the front in fading red capitals was: *Predhammer's Encyclopedia of the Supernatural.*

"Ok, so describe what it looks like," Stephanie said.

Melinda yawned and rubbed her throbbing temples. "It's like a shadow, with white eyes."

"So, it's a *black* ghost."

"I guess."

Stephanie opened to the index and ran her finger down a column of small and deeply embossed print, then turned to another page and began to read.

"Black Ghosts *are the inverse of common ghosts, or 'spirits' of the dead, which are typically white and either orb-shaped or misty and vaguely anthropoid in appearance. Unlike their white counterparts,* black ghosts *are not human in origin, although they commonly assume human form. They are believed to be the physical personification of malevolence, however their origin and modus operandi are still subjects hotly debated amongst paranormalists.*

"*Contrary to a* passive haunt—*defined as the trace energy of a deceased individual which lingers in spirit form*—a black ghost *is an* active haunt *which seeks to possess a living individual through whom it may carry out its ill intentions. This makes black ghosts much more dangerous than garden variety passive apparitions, which appear at random and for reasons unknown. Attempting to interact with a* black ghost *is highly discouraged, since their nature is not fully understood.* See Also 'POLTERGEIST, NEGATIVE.'"

"What's a 'Negative?'"

Stephanie was already searching, gently turning each page as if it were a precious primary source document. She fine-tuned the search, came to it, and flinched. Melinda slid her chair around beside her friend, looking at the definition at which Stephanie was pointing. There was an image beneath it; a photo of a man in a dark room taking a picture of himself in a mirror. A firework-burst of camera flash illuminated the man's reflection. His skin was coal black, his lips white and parted in an elongated grin. A long, maggot-white tongue jutted out between black teeth. Melinda read the passage aloud:

"A Negative (also known as a Mirror Ghost) is a sub-classification of black ghost known to be the most devious and lethal of all malicious supernatural manifestations. Negatives are shapeshifters, semi-human in form with frightening features (changeable, depending upon the particular fears of the unfortunate individual to whom it has attached itself), but may also assume a smoky, cloud-like form when moving between portals. Flat black and wooly in appearance, Negatives give off a palpable static electricity and are most powerful when within mirrors, where they have the ability to make visual the greatest fears and hatreds of their victims. Once got, a Negative is nearly impossible to rid oneself of."

Melinda looked up from the page. "That's it, Steph. That's what it is." She glanced down again. Now definition had changed.

I am you not any ghost I am you not any ghost I am you not any ghost
I am you not any ghost I am you not any ghost I am you not any ghost
I am you not any ghost I am you not any ghost I am you not any ghost
I am you not any ghost I am you not any ghost I am you not any ghost
I am you not any ghost I am you not any ghost I am you not any ghost
I am you not any ghost I am you not any ghost I am you not any ghost

Melinda shrieked and pushed the book away—it slid off the table and struck a shelf. There was a dry cracking sound as the binding tore away from the cover. Stephanie was on the floor at once, scooping up the fragile thing like a pet that had just been hit by a car.

"I'm sorry, Steph!" Melinda said, kneeling beside her. "Those words—you saw them, right?"

Stephanie only looked at her, the cover of *Predhammer's Encyclopedia of the Supernatural* dangling over her arm attached now by only a few threads.

◊

Melinda passed the rest of the school day in a state of silent terror. Everywhere she looked, things were *wrong*. Worst was during fifth period when her Algebra teacher's fingers grew long and black and pointed like crab legs as he wrote on the chalk board. Tyson found her in the hall at the end of the day and offered to give her a ride home. The familiarity of him made the horrors of the day less real. She didn't want to go home yet and asked him to pull off at the nature preserve that butted up against her back yard. They kissed for a while. She let him put his hand under her shirt, and this time didn't stop him when he slid it into her underwear. She moved across the seat and unzipped his fly.

Tyson moaned, same as Melinda had heard him doing in the mirror. A fierce jealousy gripped her suddenly. *Me, not you, Alicia*, she thought. She had the mad urge to go down on him, hard, and do more than that—to bite and wrench at him like a wolf wresting an arm from its kill. Tyson's mouth was against her cheek, his breath hot in her ear. His fingers moved in her, deeper, faster, *deeper*. His tongue was on her face, slick and long, lapping from chin to forehead, now probing her ear. It broke her from her swoon. She looked up, into the face from the mirror. The white tongue flickered out of a jack-o'-lantern mouth. The lightening eyes flashed things, terrible things. Melinda pulled away, screaming. She grabbed the door handle, got it open, fell out of the truck and ran into the woods.

It was after her immediately; a shard figure covered in black velveteen like fur. She glanced back once, saw it bounding, almost dancing, over the deadfalls and forest scrub. She could hear it speaking to her without speaking, a grating mental buzz-cabling the same message again and again like an electric shock to her brain: I AM YOU NOT ANY GHOST.

Melinda pushed through the woods, saw her house only fifty yards away. She ran across her backyard, got the key in the door and slammed it behind her. For a full minute she stood there, gasping, waiting for the doorknob to start turning. Nothing happened. She put an eye to the peephole and looked through, expecting to see that slimy tongue slapping against it. But there was only the lawn and the trees beyond. Then she heard something upstairs, a swooshing sound like someone pacing up in the hall.

"Dad?"

No answer. Melinda moved through the dining room and into the kitchen. The sound became quicker, more deliberate, closing in. *Swish swosh, swishswosh, swishswoshswishswosh.* She heard her bedroom door open.

Melinda willed her legs up the stairs and down the hall, through a thin and whirling black fog that hung in the air like shredded gauze. For a minute, she panicked—*there's a fire*—but the stuff was cool and scentless and was moving into her room only. She pushed the door open. The fog was thick but clearing, disappearing beneath the covered mirror. She watched until the last wisp had vanished under the blanket, then she walked across the room, pulled it off and looked at herself.

Her face was normal, but something was wrong in the reflection of her painting. It was no longer the happy springtime scene she'd rendered in acrylic, but a dim and snow-less winter. There were ominous scorched patches on the brown grass, and strange shriveled fruit dangled from the rotten trees. The revelers lay along the cracked flagstone walk, their faces distorted and black-lipped, blood leaking from their ears and noses. The little stone bridge had crumbled and fallen into the foul moat where more bodies floated, nibbled by pointy-toothed fish. The castle itself was an abject ruin. The turret tops were wind-worn and crumbling and lined with vultures instead of pennants. From one of the black windows, Melinda saw the face with the holographic eyes leering out at her, its stretched mouth upturned, jagged.

The Negative came out of the castle, its legs moving like a pair of scissors. It spanned the moat in one gigantic step and started up the path, impaling the bodies with its spade-shaped feet. Green matter jetted from one dead man's mouth and landed in the hair of another. The Negative plucked a piece of "fruit" with its long, crab-like fingers. Blood poured from its mouth as it bit, coursing down its velvety body and shining like burnished ebony where the red fluid ran. The fruit twitched in its hand. Melinda saw that it was a human heart, and that all of the objects in the branches were similar horrors: assorted organs and viscera dripping onto the desiccated ground.

The figure was in foreground now, the face only inches from hers, and suddenly it was *her* face, the shades of her flesh and eyes inverted. She looked at those lightning-bright portals, and in them saw her father pulling into the driveway, getting out of his car, coming into the house. She saw herself crouching at her door, waiting.

Melinda picked up the pestle out of the mortar sitting on her painting table and fired it at the mirror, shattering it save for a large guillotine-like section still attached to a corner of the mahogany frame. Downstairs, the front door opened and closed.

"Mel? You home?" She could hear in three words that he was drunk again.

*I am you. I am you, I am you* the voice purred. It wasn't static anymore, but clear, soothing, reassuring, in unison with her thoughts.

Her father was staggering up the stairs, now approaching her room. "I want to talk about the mirror. I want to say I'm sorry Mel." He was weepy and his words were slurry. It made her want to wretch. *Lousy fucking drunk*, Melinda thought.

"I'm so sorry for always blaming *you*. Can we talk?"

Melinda plucked the remaining blade of glass from the mirror frame and started toward the door. "Sure dad."

# DON'T GET TATTOOS FROM STRANGE GIRLS AT PARTIES

Monsters have populated the human imagination for millenia. We've always seen vampires in the shadows and serpents in the sea. Of course, we live in rational times now, and we know that monsters don't exist. Right?

But what if, once upon a time, they roamed the world? What if they just got old and died when man was still young? And what if they could be reborn if given rotten enough soil to grow in?

# DON'T GET TATTOOS FROM STRANGE GIRLS AT PARTIES

Danny sat backward on the folding chair, his bare chest pressed against the backrest. Despite the loud music and the ambient noise of the party, he could still hear the buzz of the tattoo gun, or maybe he just felt the vibrations in his spine and the sound was in his head.

"Feels like a lot of sweeping lines. What are you putting on me?"

"You get what you get," The tattoo artist was a lean woman named Autumn with ropy muscles, asymmetric white hair, and an indeterminate accent. She was something of an underground legend—this traveling tattoo artist with no shop or web presence. She didn't go to conventions or do interviews in magazines. She just showed up places.

No one got to pick their tattoos with Autumn. She followed her muse and you were stuck with whatever she came up with. That was her rule.

"I hope you're as good as everyone says you are."

Autumn didn't reply, but her needle dug into his spine, a bit too hard. He gritted his teeth, then wiped a tear from his eye that he hoped no one had seen. Girls generally liked talking to him. He was good-looking and charming, in a white trash kind of way. You can't win 'em all, he supposed.

Seeing that Autumn had no interest in a conversation, Danny turned his attention to his friend Clark, who sat across from him, nursing a Corona.

"You up next?"

"Nope," Clark said. "My girl will kill me if I come home with a new tattoo when the rent is already late."

"It's free, man. Autumn doesn't believe in art for money, ain't that right?" Autumn jabbed him and grunted.

"Nothing in this world is free," Clark said. "How's Nat gonna feel about you coming home with a new backpiece?"

"Like I care. She probably won't even notice. I can't even remember the last time we fucked."

"You still thinking of breaking up with her?"

"Yeah. I just need to find the right time. It's tough when she's sick like this. She's got lupus, and the doctors are pretty sure there's something else going on, but they can't figure it out. It sucks for her, but I didn't sign up for this, you know?"

"That's cold, man."

Danny rapped on the backrest of the chair, right over his heart.

"Ice cold, baby."

Clark laughed and shook his head, nearly choking on his beer. Danny let out a half-hearted snicker. Autumn stayed silent and continued with his tattoo.

0

Danny held his phone up in front of him, looking in his front-facing camera and trying to catch the angle so he could see his back in the mirror behind him. The medicine cabinet was filthy, covered in toothpaste spatters, dried shaving cream, and indeterminate grime. It was hard to catch the details of the twisted serpent that ran up and down his spine—the fine lines of the scales and the grayscale shading.

He snapped a few pictures, hoping that his incessantly shaking hands would stay still enough to capture a decent image.

The first few were too blurry, but the third was clear, aside from the filth of splatters on the mirror. Danny zoomed in, admiring the work. It was impressive—a whole different caliber than the Hampton Beach *Tattoosday* specials that covered his arms. There was a photo-realism to it, and the expert shading gave the illusion of depth.

Danny wouldn't have chosen a snake, had Autumn given him any input. He felt no special affinity with them, nor was there any emotional backstory, but the same could be said for the naked devil-girl on his forearm and the tribal ink on his shoulder. All that mattered was that it looked cool, and he most certainly thought it did.

Nat needed a stool to bathe these days, and it sat in the middle of the shower. He pushed it to the far end of the tub and turned on the faucet. He didn't bother to clean the hair out of the drain or off the wall. The water, milky white from soap scum and globs of spilled shampoo, quickly filled up around his ankles. He grabbed the largest sliver from the soapdish and scraped some white scum against the ceramic before lathering up.

The water wasn't very hot, as he didn't want to put too much stress on his healing back, but it still hurt a little. It wasn't a terrible pain, and honestly, he kind of liked it. It reminded him of pressing on a cut or running a tongue canker against your teeth. There was a certain satisfaction to it.

The pain in his back shifted around his spine like the tattoo was sliding around on his skin. It was a strange sensation and most certainly all in his head. Too much beer. Not enough sleep.

After a few minutes under the water, Danny stepped out of the shower and dried off with a musky towel. He gave it a sniff and decided to keep the dirty cloth away from his back, for fear of infection.

After patting down his back with some balled-up toilet paper, he tried to steal a glimpse of the tattoo in the mirror again, but the bathroom was too fogged up. He pulled an old tube of Aquaphor from the medicine cabinet. He'd need to cover the new tattoo in the lotion, but there was no way he could reach all of it on his own.

He grabbed the bottle and headed to the bedroom. The house was a maze of trash—the leaning tower of dishes in the kitchen sink—aluminum cans and plastic bottles littering the tables and floors—stacks of pizza boxes and unopened mail. During the best of times, he and Nat had been shit at housekeeping. Now that she was sick, the house looked like an episode of *Hoarders*.

Nat was asleep with her phone loosely hanging from her grip. He'd expected this. She was almost always asleep, and when she wasn't she was glued to her screen. He tried not to blame her. He knew she was tired and in pain. Her joints were swollen and her skin was splotchy with rashes. There were a whole host of other rotating symptoms too. One treatment would cure her fevers, then a kidney issue would pop up. It was like musical sickness.

"Nat." He sat down on the bed and brushed her hair away from her face. It was so much thinner than it used to be. "Nat, wake up for a sec."

She opened her eyes, just a tiny bit, and looked at him through the slits. He wondered if she was tired, in pain, or if the light was too much for her. Maybe she was just too depressed to bother giving the world more than a sliver of a glance.

"Nat, I need your help up for a minute."

When they had first got together Danny couldn't get over how gorgeous she was—thick wavy hair, piercing green eyes, and generous curves. She had certainly been the hottest chick he'd ever been with. It was a bonus that she had self-esteem issues, and Danny had taken full advantage of that. He'd never studied psychology, but he had an instinctive talent for landing girls with emotional issues. Backhanded compliments. Acting hot and cold with no seeming cause. Always making her wait for responses to her texts and calls. He didn't know why any of that worked on damaged girls, but they ate it up and Nat was no different.

Of course, things changed when she got sick. She needed more from him, now. He couldn't disappear for days at a time because he needed to take her to the hospital, cook her meals and make sure she got her meds. They couldn't go on road trips or go to shows, couldn't party on the weekends or have sex all night long. Their bedroom had gone from a pleasure palace to a prison cell.

Danny felt bad for her, truly, but he didn't know how much longer he could do this. She was needy and miserable. He was resentful and angry. It wasn't his fault she was sick. God had dealt her a shit hand, but that didn't mean he had to fold as well.

"Can you help me with this? I just need you to put this lotion on my back."

"I don't feel good, Danny," She mumbled, and rolled over. Her phone buzzed and she glanced at her notifications before closing her eyes again.

Danny felt a surge of anger slither up his spine. She was really just going to roll over like that? After everything, he did for her? After all he sacrificed to take care of her? And she couldn't even rub some lotion on his back?

"Fuck it," Danny whispered. He tried his best to get the lotion on himself, but he could tell that he'd missed big sections in the middle of his back. This simply wasn't a self-service kind of job.

He fumed for a few moments more about Nat refusing to help him. He looked down at her thinning hair and her splotchy skin. This wasn't what he wanted.

"Nat,' He said, ready to rip off the Band-Aid. "Nat?"

She was already asleep again. He sighed, determined to break up with her tomorrow.

0

*Danny floated through the cold and the dark. His movements were fluid but sluggish. His body felt enormous, impossibly so, as if it stretched on for miles. Twisting between sunken mountains, he cast titanic shadows over forgotten cities claimed by the depths.*

*Burning fatigue beset his ancient muscles and a heavy fog clouded his mind. He moved through the water, fueled by hunger, instinct, and rage of such intensity that it might qualify as an emotion completely distinct from human anger.*

*He dived, deeper into the ocean, past aquatic volcanos, spewing glowing lava into the black water. The heat stirred something in his mind—slippery memories of magic and fire—shadow images of a father whose face he'd forgotten long ago. Most of his memories were like that—fleeting phantasms which, as mercy would have it, only plagued him for moments at a time. Most of his existence was simply haze and hunger.*

*The other creatures of the sea, from prawns so minute they barely caught his eyes, to squids of Kraken proportions and whales the size of leviathans fled as he approached. He opened his maw and swallowed them whole. This brought him no joy, nor did it sate his incredible appetite. His hunger was as fathomless as his twisting mass.*

◊

Danny opened his eyes and found himself awake in the world of air and light, unencumbered by the monstrous mass he'd carried in the dream. He could feel Nat beside him, his back pressed against hers. She felt frail and bony. Her touch brought to mind the prawn from his dream—insignificant, chitinous pests.

It was an unfair thought. He shook his head, trying to banish that bit of cruelty from his mind, but his neck was stiff and ached at the movement. He rolled over and agony radiated out from his spine and into the muscles of his back. He gasped, but the pain robbed him of breath. Nat rolled over and looked at him with tired eyes. She asked if he was okay, but he couldn't speak.

"Danny?" Her voice was soft and weak, with an undercurrent of concern. "What's wrong?"

"My back ..." His voice was barely a whisper.

"You got a new tattoo." There was disappointment in her voice, or perhaps sadness. "It looks infected."

Danny swore under his breath and forced himself into a sitting position. He couldn't manage to straighten his back, so he sat hunched over and struggled to breathe through the pain. He thought about the idea of infection, and he could suddenly feel lines of heat under his skin following the twisting body of the serpent on his back. Of course, it was infected. He'd gotten the tattoo for free from some artsy weirdo at a party. Who knew if that chick was even who she'd claimed to be. Autumn was a legend. No one knew what she looked like, and anyone could claim to be her.

"It's huge," Nat muttered. "How much did it cost?"

"That's your concern right now?" Danny snapped. "The damn money?"

"No, I just ..."

Danny waved his hand and huffed, cutting her off. He gritted his teeth and forced himself out of bed. The pain in his back was intense—up there with the worst of migraines or that time he'd had an abscess in his molar. He needed to go to the doctor and get the tattoo checked out. Even if it wasn't infected and he just slept funny, they could give him something for the pain.

"Danny, I wasn't trying to give you a hard time."

Danny didn't have the patience to argue with Nat about the tattoo or what she did or didn't mean. He hobbled to a pile of clothes in the corner and pieced together an outfit. She tried to engage him again as he struggled to get dressed, but he asked her to please stop talking. He was afraid he'd blurt everything out and break up with her then and there, but he knew this wasn't the time. He couldn't do it when he was out of his mind in pain. It had to be when they were both lucid and reasonable.

Nat sniffled and picked up her phone. She started scrolling and typing. Danny left for the emergency room, and neither of them said goodbye.

◊

"Beautiful work, but it's definitely infected," the doctor said, pressing a finger against Danny's back. It hurt and Danny let out a sharp breath between clenched teeth.

"Hopefully it was just something environmental. I doubt it was a problem with the needle or the ink, but we'll take blood tests to make sure there isn't anything else going on. I'll give you antibiotics to clear it up and a little something for the pain."

Danny was hoping for Vicodin or Codeine, but his guess was he'd get a script for extra strength ibuprofen or something. He'd take a look at the prescription and maybe he could nudge the doctor toward something better if that was the case.

"My bigger concern than the tattoo is your spine, however. It looks like you have some severe scoliosis going on. Has anyone diagnosed you about that before?"

"What? No. I've never had back issues." His back throbbed even as he spoke.

"Sit up straight for me, as straight as you can."

Danny tried, but his spine wouldn't respond. He could feel the arch of his torso, crooked and uneven. The doctor pressed on his back, nudging him upright and pain shot through his core. Just like when he'd tried to get up from bed, his chest tightened and he found it a struggle to breathe.

"Well, this sort of thing doesn't just happen overnight. You need to go see your primary care and get your back looked at. This could end up being a real problem."

Danny tried to nod, but it was too painful to commit to the motion.

◊

Danny sat on the bus, hunched over on the back row of seats, his hood thrown over his head. His eyelids kept closing on their own accord, then fluttering open with each turn and jerky stop. He must have slept worse than he'd realized.

His mind was foggy and each time he dozed off, he'd fall into a shallow dream where he swam through oceanic canyons and underwater mountains crumbled to sand beneath his weight. The fleeting dreams held more than just forests of kelp and glimpses of sunken civilizations, however. There were feelings in the dream—tangible sensations and emotions. Anger, focused and honed to a razor-sharp arrowhead. Exhaustion, both physical and mental, forged from a life that spanned time in proportion to the way stars span the void of space. Emptiness and hunger like a blackhole within, yearning for light and life, but never sated.

The bus came to a sudden stop. Danny jerked forward and opened his eyes. A little boy held on to his mother's purse and stared at him. The boy wore an unusual expression. Danny couldn't figure out if he was afraid, intrigued, or disgusted. Maybe it was all three.

He stuck his tongue out at the child. The boy flinched, then buried his face into his mother's sweater. Danny laughed to himself. The boy's fear amused him, but also it made him hungry—not in any way he had known before—but in a deep, metaphysical manner that he couldn't quite understand.

The blue awning for the pizza place at the end of his street was visible through the windshield of the bus. Danny pressed the button to signal that he wanted to get off at the next stop. It took an effort to stand, and the pain in his back radiated through his butt and down his thighs. He stumbled forward, nearly falling, and grasped onto one of the poles for balance.

No one offered him help or even a word of sympathy. They looked at him with disgust or suspicion—like he was a leper or a junky. People squished together to avoid his touch. They stared at their phones and the floor in an effort not to make eye contact.

The bus came to a halt and Danny hobbled down the two steps to the rear door. Each step felt like an eternity. He could hear other passengers sighing with impatience, even as he hissed out his pain between clenched teeth.

The short walk from the bus stop to his house was hard and agonizing. He stopped several times to lean against light posts and street signs. It hurt to breathe too deeply, so he took shallow breaths, but the occasional sharp gasp would send a pulse of agony through his body.

With much effort, he made it home. The mailbox was overflowing and a post-it note attached to it read "please take your mail!". He plucked the note up, crumpled it into a ball, and tossed it into the dead grass.

He fumbled for his keys, and they fell from his hand. Looking down, he knew that he wouldn't be able to bend down to retrieve them. Nonetheless, he tried. His aching back resisted, sending painful protestations up and down his spine. He could maybe balance himself against the door and kneel, but he was afraid he wouldn't be able to get up.

He looked at the doorbell but knew it wouldn't help. Nat wouldn't get up to answer the door for some stranger, and she would have no reason to think it was Danny. He pulled out his phone and called her instead. She answered on the second ring, much faster than he had expected.

"Hello?"

"Nat, I dropped my keys, and I can't bend to get them. Can you let me in?"

She let out a long sigh. Danny didn't know if it was from her fatigue, from the thought of what pain might come from getting out of bed, or from general annoyance at him. Whatever the reason, it sparked his impatience.

"Please, Nat. I'm in a lot of pain."

"Sure. Just give me a minute."

She hung up the phone without saying goodbye, which was odd for her. Then again, she was going to see him in just a minute, so maybe it wasn't so odd. Perhaps he was reading into things because of the foul mood he was in.

Danny leaned against the doorframe and rested his head against his forearm. Something stirred in the bushes—a squirrel or a bunny. He didn't care to turn and look, but his muscles spasmed and his spine wriggled at the sound. The pain was so intense that he fell to the ground, wailing like a child. He could feel his backbone writhing beneath his muscle and flesh—pushing against his skin as it lurched in a serpentine fashion.

Through tear-blurred eyes, Danny could see a rabbit dart out of the bushes dash and across the street. A few seconds late it was gone, vanished down a neighbor's driveway. Once the animal was out of sight, his spasms slowed, then stopped. His back still ached, so much worse than it had before, but the impossible agony of a few moments before was fading.

Nat opened the door and gasped at Danny's prone form. He looked at her and wept, unable to form words. Weak as she was, she knelt beside him, then helped him inside. Sick herself, Nat stumbled alongside him as they navigated their way from the front door to the bedroom. They bumped into furniture, knocking over stacks of takeout boxes and pyramids of empty cans.

Danny caught his foot in a pile of dirty clothes just inside the bedroom and fell. He swore and cried and slammed his fist against the floor. Nat gave him a minute. She knew from experience that he might need it.

Once he was calm and she had him settled on the bed, she stroked his hair and held his hand, and asked him what was wrong. He looked at her and for the first time in months, she looked gorgeous to him. She didn't seem like this emaciated, dwindling burden of a person. She looked strong and sweet and full of confident beauty.

"You're wearing makeup," he said, a look of confusion mixed with the pain written on his face.

She ignored his statement and asked what was wrong with him. He didn't have an answer, so he simply broke down into tears.

0

Danny hadn't slept in weeks. Not really. He drifted in and out of consciousness, splitting his time between hazy dreams of dark waters and hours of prescription inebriation. The doctors couldn't figure out what was wrong with him, so they'd prescribed him Oxys in the meantime. It took the edge off, but the pain never retreated very far.

He flipped through the pictures on his phone, the ones he'd asked Nat to take. The tattoo on his back looked different in each one. Its position constantly shifted, bending his spine along with it. It had grown as well, longer and fatter—taking up more of his flesh for itself.

Nat and all the doctors told him it was his imagination. If the tattoo looked different, it was because his twisting spine was distorting it, not the other way around. Danny knew the truth—he could feel the thing on his back, moving beneath his skin—the sensation of its heartbeat and the ripple of its serpentine muscles.

Nat wasn't in bed with him. She hardly ever was anymore. He didn't know if she was feeling better, but she had certainly taken up the slack since his back problems started. Sure, the house was still a pit, but she'd stepped up and taken care of him through all of this, despite her lupus and whatever other illnesses they'd yet to diagnose her with. She was a hell of a woman, and he couldn't believe he'd ever planned on leaving her.

She was taking better care of herself too. He didn't have to harass her about taking showers. She was getting dressed in real clothes and putting on makeup. She was acting alive again, even if it was clear how hard it was for her to do so.

Nat's phone buzzed on her nightstand, rattling her pill bottles. He looked over, thinking it was kind of odd. She never let go of the thing and he wondered where she'd gone off to without it.

It buzzed again, two more times in quick succession. He tried to roll over so he could reach it and see why it was going off, but it hurt too much to move.

The bedroom door opened, as far as it could with the pile of laundry behind it, and Nat squeezed her way inside. Her hair was wet from the shower, and he could catch the curve of her thighs from underneath her towel. She'd just laid there in bed for so many months, scrolling her phone and waiting for death, that he'd forgotten how beautiful she was. He wanted to tell her, but he liked to save compliments for more strategic times. If you just told a woman she was gorgeous whenever the thought came to mind, you'd lose all the power in the relationship—at least that's what experience had taught him.

"Your phone's been buzzing." His voice was soft, muted by pain and exhaustion.

Nat picked up her phone and swiped the screen. A smile crossed her face as she read the message. It wasn't the kind of smirk someone gets from a meme or a cute animal video. It was wide and full of life—the look of a woman in love.

"Who are you talking to?"

Danny realized he had never asked her that, not in all the months she'd been sick, living life through her phone. He'd figured she'd been scrolling through social media or taking dumb online quizzes, but what if there had been someone on the other side that whole time?

Nat took a moment to respond. The smile stayed on her face up until she took her eyes off the screen. With squinted eyes and a look of faux indifference, she told him it was no one.

"Bullshit. Let me see your phone."

"Um, no," she said, placing it down on the dresser on the other side of the room.

Danny looked at it from the bed, far away from his reach. He grew furious and his back spasmed. He asked her again who she was talking to, anger in his voice. She sighed and fished out clothes from the dresser with her back turned to him.

"You don't know him."

"Some dude? Are you cheating on me?"

Nat dropped her towel and put on her bra and panties. Once she was covered up, she walked over to the bed and sat beside Danny. She placed her hand on top of his.

"I didn't want to do it like this, Danny." His heart was racing, and the room began to spin. "I was going to tell you, but I wanted to make sure you were all set up first, that you had someone to help you out."

"Are you kidding me?"

"I know it's shitty, but we haven't been in love for a long time."

"I took care of you!" he hissed through gritted teeth. "I cooked and paid the bills and took you to doctors for all those months you just laid there waiting to die. And now you're just gonna walk out on me?"

"You did take care of me, and I will never forget that, but I'm still sick, Danny, and I'm probably going to die. I want to be happy again before I do. And this ..." she said, gesturing to his twisted body. "I'm just not equipped for it."

Danny began to cry, and shake. He grasped her hand and squeezed it hard. His spine wriggled angrily beneath his tattoo.

"I love you, Nat!"

"No, you don't. You're just scared."

0

Danny's sheets were stained with piss and shit. His shirt was stuck to his back with dried pus from the infection of the growing tattoo. His belly rumbled and he couldn't remember the last time he'd eaten.

No one came to see him after Nat left. If she'd called a social worker or a nurse or who the hell ever, they never showed up. None of his friends had either. Clark and the rest of his buddies were happy to show up and drink his beer or smoke his weed, but they weren't so interested in things like helping someone move or driving them to the hospital.

He'd tried to call Nat a few times. More than a few, really. One time a guy answered, warning him not to call back. Soon after that, she'd blocked his number.

Now his phone was dead, and he couldn't even move to plug it in. He didn't care to, either. Nat and all his fair-weather friends—his life of parties, chicks, and booze—none of that held any interest to him anymore. It didn't even seem real. Only three desires remained. One was for his agony to end. The second was for the soothing touch of frigid waters. The last was to eat—to consume any life that passed his way.

His arms and legs hung limp and useless, his torso curled into a crumpled ball. The snake on his back writhed, more furiously by the hour. His spine followed each move of the tattoo, twisting back and forth, wriggling beneath his skin. Ribs cracked in his chest, sheering away from his backbone. Organs ruptured against flailing vertebrae.

When he felt the flesh on his back tear, it was almost a relief. The sound was nearly as bad as the pain—the ripping of flesh and the clacking of bones. Violent spasms gripped him as his spine broke away from his skull, tore itself from his body and slithered out from under his shirt. The runaway backbone carried his consciousness and his infected tattoo with it.

Danny's upper vertebrae popped and cracked, reforming into the arrowhead skull of a serpent. The tattooed skin wrapped itself around his dismembered spine, knitting itself back together. The ink coalesced into slick scales that overtook the human flesh. Muscles and cartilage grew around his spine, firming up his deflated form. Eyes coalesced in his skull and organs grew beneath his skin.

From his new body, he looked at the flesh he'd left behind. It was an empty and lifeless thing—a molted husk. He gave it no more thought than any skin he'd ever shed in an incredibly long life.

The snake slithered out of the bedroom, through the maze of trash and filth that was Danny's apartment, snatching up flies and vermin along the way. His hunger was incredible, and these tiny pests would not satisfy it. He needed to move to better hunting grounds where larger prey might be had.

The further he moved from the eviscerated body in the bedroom, the less familiar things looked. He flicked his tongue and picked up the bitter smell of old beer, but it brought him no memories or emotions. He could sense electricity coursing through boxes of plastic and steel, but he couldn't conceive the purpose of such contraptions.

He followed the smell of life and warm blood through a hole in the kitchen. Behind the wall, he found a den made up of paper trash, stained with mammalian piss and dotted with tiny pellets of excrement. A litter of hairless mammals huddled in the filthy scraps, their mother squeaking in terror. He struck forth and devoured the mother, then her children.

The smell of fresh air wafted in beyond the mammals' den. He followed the scent outside into a yard dotted with tufts of tall grass. He maneuvered around sun-bleached Budweiser cans and shards of amber glass that jutted out of the soil like the ruins of a tiny city lost to the ravages of time.

Beyond the fence line lay a small stream. He wriggled between the chain link and made his way to the rocky shore. He plunged into the water. It was cold and it felt like home.

As he swam down the stream, he could not remember how he'd come to be in this place, or where he even was. He could not recall Nat, or Clint, or even the name of that wretched mammal he had just freed himself from.

The last thing he could remember was resting his head on a rocky shore in some land far to the north. His age and his size had become a burden. He'd grown so old and tired. That's when the girl came. She called herself Autumn and she'd come to kill him.

The girl had jabbed something into his eye—a thin, wicked blade, dripping black—and he'd been powerless to defend himself. Her touch was soft and kind, and she'd waited with him as death approached. She'd whispered sweet words and promises of resurrection as she stroked his enormous head.

She delivered on her promise. He was no longer old and infirm. His mind was not slowed by the fog of millennia. Jörmungandr was reborn.

# CONTAINERS

There are lots of different "containers", aren't there? They hold all sorts of things. This one I'm working on, for instance, will contain something — or, someone, rather — before the lid's nailed on. Anyone who might choose to open it later will find... well...

Young Tonya doesn't like going to Grandma's house. It's like being entombed in trash, and there are secrets — horrifying ones — stacked amongst it. That harrowing tome, the Predhammer's Encyclopedia of the Supernatural, makes another appearance here, as does another form of "black ghost"

— one born of nightmares and stored in butter tubs.

# CONTAINERS

Tonya didn't like going to Grandma's. She lived in a scab-colored ranch in the center of an overgrown field that was feral with rodents and surrounded by a perimeter of diseased ash trees Grandpa had planted forty-five years earlier. Grandpa had died the same year Tonya's father was born. The neighboring farms, with their grayed skeleton barns and homesteads, had been abandoned years ago, left to disintegrate into the rich black earth that hadn't been tilled for planting in two generations.

Tonya once heard her father refer to Grandma as a "hoarder." When she asked him what this meant, he told her that it was a person who liked to "save stuff." Grandma, Tonya guessed, must have been an extreme hoarder since she saved *everything*. All the rooms in her house were packed near to the ceiling with a lifetime of accretion. Even her trash never seemed to leave, rather it got moved to the garage (apparently Grandpa's car was buried somewhere beneath). The stuff was beginning to encroach into the "walks" as Grandma called them—the narrow paths that snaked through the mass of mess.

Lately Tonya had been coming to Grandma's a lot. Her parents had recently divorced; she only saw her father every other weekend, and though he was supposed to be spending the time with her, he invariably dumped Tonya off at Grandma's so that he could get drunk and bring that *woman* back to his tiny post-separation apartment. It was the same routine every weekend. Reeking of cologne, he would pick Tonya up at her mother's, drive her to the nearest fast food restaurant and buy her whatever she wanted. While she ate, he talked or texted on his phone, occasionally tossing out a distracted inquiry about school, and responding blandly and in delay to her replies. Next, they went to a department store, where Tonya picked out "a present." "Anything for my favorite girl," he'd always say. She had to admit that in the beginning she had liked this part, but after months of such déja vu weekends it only made her sad now. Tonya had every doll she wanted (even the really expensive ones she would have never gotten before the divorce) and besides, she was starting to outgrow dolls. The last two weekends her father hadn't even come into the store with her. He'd dropped her off out front, given her his credit card and waited in the car while Tonya wandered around inside, deciding which object would serve as a proxy for his attention that week.

On this most recent Saturday, after fruitlessly perusing the toy department, Tonya went to look at the books and magazines, hoping the store had the latest Carla Clueless detective story (she'd read all nineteen previous installments). She saw volumes two, nine, thirteen, and fourteen, but alas, no magic number twenty. As she was turning to leave, another book caught her eye: a large tome, bound in white leather. *Predhammer's Encyclopedia of the Supernatural* read the big crimson capitals on the cover. It was weighty; Tonya had to half cradle it against her body in order to peruse it. A thrill ran through her as she flipped through the pages. They were full black and white photographs of ghosts—*real* ghosts, supposedly—and illustrations of creatures and weird, eerie settings among the rows and rows of small print. Tonya considered herself more of a mysteries girl, but she found herself intensely drawn to what she was seeing. Maybe it was because it was a book for adults rather than kids. Or maybe there was something familiar about it, something necessary in the pages—a connection made in her mind which she *felt* but could not explain. It was an odd feeling, a sort of disembodied intuition that seemed to be speaking to her from a part of her mind that she only heard from when it involved danger.

The book cost more than double what her father usually allowed her to spend. *Anything for his favorite girl,* she thought with a smile as she closed the tome with a resounding and satisfying *whomph* and carried it to the checkout counter. Back in the car, Tonya handed her father the receipt and his credit card. As he was putting the latter back in his wallet he glanced at the little slip of paper and frowned, first at the book and then at Tonya. He said nothing as he drove out of the lot, and for a few minutes Tonya reveled in her small victory.

But her feeling of triumph faded, replaced with that familiar foreboding as soon as she saw the ramshackle façade of Grandma's house, with its tomb-like front door and windows lidded with jaundiced shades. Looking at the place through the windshield of her father's new truck (a divorce present to himself) Tonya realized how wrong it was that he was leaving her here, even if it was his own mother's house.

Recently, Grandma had been getting the horrors.

She looked at her father and saw that he was smiling. *He's already at the bar,* she thought. And she knew what he was going to say next. *Have fun with your Grandma and tell her I said hello,* followed by the false promise of breakfast together the following morning (it had yet to happen) before he drove her back to her mother's. Invariably he had picked her up around three the next day, puffy eyed, his breath like something curdled, and the shadow of a certain cloying perfume on his clothes (the same polo and jeans he'd been wearing he'd dropped her off the night before).

Now, as he pulled up in front of the windowless garage door, dented and foxed with rust, Tonya blurted: "Dad, I don't want to stay at Grandma's tonight."

"Daddy has plans ..."

"Aren't your plans supposed to be with me?"

"But we just *spent* time together, didn't we?" he said, gripping Tonya's shoulder and giving it a little convincing shake. "I took you for a nice lunch and bought you a ... that ... thing you wanted ..."

"What I really want is to stay with you. I don't like Grandma's."

"I'm sorry, honey. Daddy has an important meeting."

Tonya knew who this "meeting" was with. She had never met the woman, but she was certain she'd recognize her perfume when she inevitably did. Her father's phone rang. Tonya heard the clink of glasses, jukebox music, shouting as he answered it. "*Hey*," he said softly. "Yeah, I am. Can you hold on a minute?" He set the phone down on his thigh and stared out at the waist-high tangle of weed and wild grass that was Grandma's front yard. The scene was electric with insect song, the stridulation of cicadas, the hinge creak of crickets. "Tonya, you're a big girl now. You understand that adults have to work in order to pay bills—*your* bills, as well as my own."

"Most adults don't work on weekends," Tonya said.

"Not true," her father replied. "*I* do. I work every day. That's how it is when you own your own business."

Tonya didn't respond. She looked into her lap where her latest present lay, and pretended to cry. Her father picked up his phone, muttered into it—"I have to call you back." He paused a moment, then said, mechanically, "I know this has been very hard on you, sweetie, all this ... going back and forth. But you know I love you very much, right?"

*Do you?* Tonya wondered. It had been nothing but pain for her and her mother these past few months, since he'd decided to leave, since *he* had caused the hurt. If people loved you, why would you treat them so awfully? But now as she looked at him, something occurred to Tonya that seemed almost incomprehensible: This whole divorce thing was actually *fun for him*. It was like a vacation from his real life—a life in which Tonya did not rank very highly. Without a word, she opened the door, grabbed her overnight bag and the big cumbersome book and edged awkwardly off the seat until her feet met gravel. Her father did not offer to help her to Grandma's front door. Instead, he uttered another of those heartless I Love Yous and gave her a vague parting smile as he reached across the seat and pulled the passenger door closed.

Tonya started slowly towards Grandma's, pausing at a crumbling concrete frog under which the house key was hidden. As she bent to pick it up, she glanced at the truck as it moved down the crushed stone drive. Her father already had the phone to his ear, and she was pretty sure she saw him grinning. The radio was on now too, the music rising as he pulled out onto the road, leaving behind a dust cloud ghost.

0

The breezeway stunk of moth balls and avian excrement. These were only the first of a bevy of smells awaiting anyone who visited Grandma. Years ago, she used to "care" for birds, until someone (most likely her own son, Tonya guessed) reported her to animal control. Now the birds were gone but the cages remained, stacked like rickety tenements and loaded with fossilized shit and desiccated seed husks. Three short stairs piled with assorted clutter led to the side door. Tonya went in, greeted not by Grandma but the stink of trapped air—a farty odor that reminded her of an old grilled cheese sandwich. Despite it being a bright summer evening, it was dim and shadowy, and the single grease-glazed bulb over the sink did little to disperse the gloom. The kitchen table on Tonya's right sagged dangerously under its burden of junk. Everywhere she looked her eyes met something shocking. A mummified apple peered at her like a shrunken head from behind a set of old-fashioned curlers. Beside this was a cup of tea, mold spots floating on the surface like lily pads. It was beginning to look like Halloween year-round at Grandma's with all the cobwebs.

Carefully Tonya stepped along one of the "walks," not much wider than herself, which cut through the walls of clutter. As Tonya approached the mouth of the hall, Grandma stepped out from the bathroom. She was a big, fleshy woman, wearing a threadbare house dress that was stained yellow at the crotch and armpits. Beneath the thin fabric Tonya could see the dark shadows of the old woman's aureoles and fat fold lines. Her hair was long and white and matted, and her black eyes were underlined in blue pencil.

"Tahhhnya … my drain's clogged. Will you help me, honey?"

"S-sure, Grandma," Tonya said. She followed the old woman into the bathroom, where several inches of brown water stood in the pale pink tub. Grandma offered an unraveled coat hanger. Tonya reluctantly set her things on a stack of rippled magazines behind the door, moved a few slow steps forward and took the length of wire. Grandma balled her fists and made a plunging gesture. Grimacing, Tonya stuck one end into the murk and fished around until she found the drain. She prodded several times, but the clog held.

Grandma fluttered her long, calcified fingernails and grinned toothlessly. "Maybe try with your fingers."

Tonya shook her head and began to back away, but Grandma gripped her by the shoulder. The nails were sharp and felt as though they would pierce through Tonya's t-shirt. "I can't bend down *Tahhhnya*, help Grandma, will you?"

Tonya knelt reluctantly beside the tub. The surface was scummy with brown foam and dotted with dead flies. It had a well water rotten egg smell, spiked with an underlying fecal stench. She held her breath, trying to suppress a mounting nausea, and stuck her hand in. The water was warmer than she'd anticipated; somehow this made it worse. *Oh god …do it quick*, she thought. Tonya fumbled for the drain, grimacing as her nails scraped thick sludge off the bottom of the tub. She opened her mouth—she thought to vomit—but instead came a long belch reeking of fast food. She turned her head to one side, looking away from the water as she continued to search. A few seconds later her fingers became entwined in a large thatch of hair hovering above the plughole. She grabbed and pulled, bringing up what looked like a drowned rat.

"Whoa, my!" Grandma exclaimed. She grabbed a metal bin painted like a candy cane, pulled the lid off and instructed Tonya to deposit the slimy mass within. The drain gurgled, burped bubbles, but the water remained. "Looks like there's more!" Grandma said anxiously. Tonya stuck her hand in again, cleared out another tangle of hair and slime and plopped it into Grandma's Christmas tin. At last, the standing water began to evacuate freely. Grandma was grinning and pawing at the goop admiringly. "Good girl. You clean up, and I'll make us some sandwiches."

When Grandma had gone Tonya went to the sink, turned on the tap and let the water run until it steamed. She picked a crusty sliver of soap off the top basin and scrubbed her hands and arms and under her nails and then dried off with a stiff towel. When she turned to gather her things, she saw the backpack lying where she'd left it but not the new book. After searching the surrounding piles, she went into the kitchen where Grandma was pulling apart filmy pieces of bologna and placing them on slices of bread laid out on VHS tapes.

"Grandma, did you take my book from the bathroom?"

"How's that?"

"I brought a book with me. A big white one with red letters."

The old woman shook her head. "Never seen it before." She picked up a butter knife and began spreading mayonnaise on the bread. "You know, you should always keep track of your things, honey. You have to have a system. I know precisely where *every single item* in this house is located," she said, jabbing the knife around at random in punctuation of each word. Grandma put one of the sandwiches on a paper plate that looked like it had been previously used for hot wings and handed it to Tonya.

Frowning, Tonya carried the plate to the three-season room at the rear of the house. The first time she'd visited Grandma's this area had been impassible, but over several weeks she had gradually made her way through to the back door—rearranging the stacks of sale papers and broken appliances and rusty ironing boards and dangerously leaning shelves loaded with long-expired canned goods until she'd reached it. Now she went outside and sat on the stoop. The grass surrounded her—three walls of yellow swaying weeds that always made her think of a picture she'd seen of Africa in one of her textbooks. She imagined a lion roaming somewhere within, imagined hearing its growl, low and ominous as it approached. Tonya sacrificed her sandwich to it and pretended that the beast was appeased. Later when she went up the stairs she did so backwards, so as to not turn her back on the yard. She didn't think there was really a lion. But it was hard to know for sure. Really, anything could have been in there.

0

There was nothing to do at Grandma's. The house had three bedrooms: a spare room that was always locked, Tonya's father's old room (where Tonya slept), and Grandma's at the end of the hall. Grandma spent all her time in her room, where the only working television was (apparently there were four others in the living room—long since piled upon). There were plenty of radios around, but Tonya had never been able to dig her way through the junk to find an outlet. So, same as every other weekend, she sat on her father's childhood bed and unpacked her bag in the stuffy silence. She seemed to bring more and more every weekend. Dolls, ponies, stuffed animals, action figures, and of course, all those kid's meal toys, which she proceeded to arrange in a circle around her. She did not play with these things anymore. They were there only for comfort—familiar faces amidst the claustrophobic world of clutter, their plastic stares keeping a protective eye on Tonya as she re-read a Carla Clueless novel and snacked on a store of crackers and candy stowed in one of the backpack pockets. She passed the remaining daylight hours like this, growing more and more anxious as the shade of the room's only window not obstructed by cardboard boxes slowly darkened.

Around midnight it would begin—long, wavering moans coming from Grandma's room, moans which gradually rose into harsh shrieks that, after a few tense moments, abruptly stopped. Next was the sound of Grandma's door opening, a series of slow and ponderous approaching footsteps, and then the grate of a key in the knob of the door across the hall. After this was a long silence, then a noise like someone tearing newspaper, and finally Grandma reemerging and returning to her room. The first time this happened Tonya had been too terrified to call out to Grandma, to see if she was okay. Tonya had shamelessly clutched a random doll to her chest and cocooned herself under the covers, remaining there until she thought she'd suffocate.

Now, as she lay waiting for Grandma to begin the bizarre ritual, Tonya found that she was curious rather than terrified. She wondered: *What does Grandma do in that room?* She wanted to know, wanted to see for herself. So, when the moans began, Tonya got out of bed and crossed the bile-colored carpet, the same her father had once padded along in his pajamas when the house had some sane semblance of order, and put her ear to the door. She heard Grandma coming, heard the key in the lock. Tonya opened her own door an inch and peeked out into the hall. The doorways were skewed from one another; the one at which Grandma stood was closer to the kitchen, so the old woman was partly lit in profile by the range hood light. Grandma disappeared into the room, and a few moments later Tonya heard a sound like newspaper being ripped. When Grandma came out of the room her eyes were streaked with long black lines. She seemed only half conscious, like a sleepwalker, as she worked the key in the lock. As she started back down the hall, passing Tonya's room in a slow and lurching gait, Tonya noticed that Grandma had not closed the door tightly before locking it.

She waited until she thought Grandma would be asleep again before stepping into the hall. Approaching the door, she heard that papery sound again, a sort of fluttering crinkle, though now that she was closer it seemed more like a flapping, like wings. Were there *birds* in there? It sort of sounded like birds, but the longer she stood listening the less it sounded like them. She went back to her room and closed the door. *It's too dark to see anything anyway*, she thought, not wanting to admit to herself how frightened she was. But the image of that un-closed door wouldn't leave her mind as she lay staring up at the dust-caked ceiling fan.

She slept intermittently, and at the earliest hint of dawn, Tonya got up and peered out into the hall. She looked at Grandma's door, then at the other one, staring for a long time before approaching it. The room was shadowy and strange, even for Grandma's house. It was silent except for that occasional papery flapping noise. A path, even narrower than the others in the house, led to the room's only window over which a brittle roller shade was drawn. The shade squealed as Tonya lifted it, letting in a sunburst swell of light. She turned around and looked at the room. There were no cages, no birds, only towers of closed containers—the taupe-colored kind that margarine came in.

*What was going on here?* Tonya picked up one of the containers. It was light—not much heavier than the plastic itself. Slowly, she peeled the lid back and peered inside. There was an odd smell that reminded her of wet charcoal and also burned hair. At the bottom she saw what appeared to be burnt paper layered like lasagna. The grayish-black matter began to expand, puffing out, its marcelled edges scampering up the slick cylindrical wall. Tonya dropped the container, shrieking as she watched the "paper" unfurl and begin to creep along the floor, making a sound like crackling—or burning?—leaves as it moved, doubling, tripling, quadrupling in size. She reeled backwards, knocking over several more towers as she lunged out into the hall and ran to Grandma's room.

She had never been in Grandma's room. Tonya found it to be a lot like the others in the house, only here the windows were covered in sheets of tin foil. Atop the vanity stood gas station soda cups, costume jewelry, cans of insecticide, piles of folded pastel sheets, a desiccated and web-festooned bouquet of roses in a teal vase, a can of government issued pork, conglomerations of perfume and pill bottles arranged like little cities. The room reeked of dirty laundry, talcum powder, incontinence. An oscillating fan set up on a chair at the end of the bed disseminated the stink. A white bulb glowed erumpent from a shadeless lamp on the nightstand. Tonya raised a hand to block the light as she looked at Grandma. The old woman lay with her hands crossed over her chest like a corpse, her breathing stertorous. Her thin nightgown was streaked with wet black. Beside her, lying open on the bed, was *Predhammer's Encyclopedia of the Supernatural,* the crimson ribbon page marker lying along the gutter like a serpentine tongue. Tonya waded around to the other side of the bed through heaps of newspaper piled against the footboard like drifted snow and squinted down at the book. On the left-hand page was the black and white photograph of a dark shape on all-fours peering at the camera from behind a door. The wide-set eyes were blazing fractured bulbs; the head was fox-shaped, but the face was flat, and the ears were shaped like bat wings. Above this figure was a word in bold type that Tonya didn't recognize—PERINOCT— and beneath it, several rows of text:

*A* PERINOCT *is an entity composed of nightmares which has the unique ability of externally manifesting itself outside its host. Unlike the early definition of nightmare, in which an outside entity in the form of an evil spirit was formerly thought to oppress individuals during sleep, a* PERINOCT *is created by the dreamer during dreaming and must be purged, usually via the mouth, ears, or nose, though in severe cases expulsion occurs through the eyes. Once expelled, a* PERINOCT *must be contained, lest it escape and torment the dreamer, resulting in hallucinations, madness, and even death. One is, however, easily managed if captured immediately after secretion (any receptacle with a sealable lid will suffice), and subsequently disposed of by burning the entire vessel. If not destroyed, the entity must be stored with care: PERINOCTs do not decompose, and have been reported to emerge from places of confinement breeched after millennia.*

*Ashy and brittle in texture while dormant to black and viscous when fully enlarged, PERINOCTs possess intuitive, even telepathic abilities, and are able to replicate and reproduce sounds and sense triggers of the dreamer. Though bound to the individual who created it, a PERINOCT is the only supernatural entity known to be communicable, and may spread to new, uninfected hosts. (Recently it has been suggested that the ability to develop a PERINOCT may be an inheritable condition, though as of the date of this publication no evidence has been provided to corroborate this claim.) A PERINOCT's ability to negatively effect the physical world makes it one of the most dangerous of the sub classification of entities known as BLACK GHOSTS and must be handled at all times with extreme care. \*Recommended immediate consultation with trained paranormalist if contracted\*.*

Tonya looked at Grandma, wondering: *Why wouldn't she have burned them?* Then she thought: Maybe this was what happened to abandoned people. They clung to every last object, everything that had once been part of them. *Things* could not choose to leave you—you could keep them, pack them in the chambers where you ate and washed and slept until they clogged your life like sclerotic arteries.

Tonya reached out and shook Grandma. The old woman's flesh was cool and damp and like biscuit dough. "Grandma?" The eyes, black and glossy as hematite, opened slowly. "I'm sorry, Grandma. I went into your room. I opened one of your containers ..."

With startling speed Grandma pushed off the bed and lunged toward the closet. She grabbed an industrial-sized box of foil from a buckling upper shelf and began tearing off sheets and stuffing them in the gap under the door. She glanced back at Tonya. "It's like a mirror. They see themselves and get confused," Grandma said, clearly though tremulously. Above the metallic crunch Tonya began to notice another sound—a crackling hiss like the rattle of a snake.

"The *vent!*" Grandma cried, thrusting a large swathe of foil at Tonya. "Under the bed—cover it, quick!"

Shaking, Tonya knelt, threw back the bed skirt and peeked below the frame. Near the wall, amidst the ancient compaction of objects and garbage, she saw a black head poking up through one of narrow slats of the heating register set in the floor. The face was flat as an ink spill. One of its ragged ears stood erect, the other hung like a broken wing. The membranous eyes were like a cracked windshield, and they seemed to bulge and pulsate as they focused on Tonya. Then, quite suddenly, it slid out from the vent, slithering towards the opposite side of the bed, up and out of site. A moment later, Grandma screamed.

Tonya drew back, partly tangled in the bed skirt. A long and oily wraith, hovering like a gulper eel, was looming over Grandma. The old woman backed into the vanity, shattering perfume bottles and knocking cups of stagnant diet cola onto the rug. A bitter, cloying stench filled the room. The Perinoct's eyes were now clear and unblemished, and full of images—horrid images, beaming like a projector into Grandma's eyes. She raised her hands, palsied and bleeding, let out a final spasmodic wail and slumped onto the floor. At the same moment the wraith began to disintegrate from the bottom up, like a burning fuse, into gray powder. The oscillating fan rotated, dispersing the ash, and Tonya coughed and gasped and the scream, when it came, was a muted, dry rattle.

It's the night before Halloween and Detroit is on fire. They call it Devil's Night. For most folks that's a figurative name, but HUNTER knows that sometimes there are real devils hiding in the shadows... even if he's the only one who can see them.

Other's might be content to give the night to the monsters, but for HUNTER October 30th is

# HUNTER'S NIGHT

# HUNTER'S NIGHT

**H**unter looked down at his work as he talked, rather than at Benny. He sat at a cluttered workbench in a derelict auto shop, rubbing canola oil into a whetstone with a faded red shop rag. The wooden-handled Bowie knife he was sharpening was an ancient thing. The weapon had been passed down in his family for generations. His great grandfather had carried it as a lawman out west. His granddad and his father had both taken it to war. Its steel had tasted the blood of thieves, fascists, and commies. It was a relic, and he took great care of it.

The two-block area around his garage was mostly abandoned. Hunter missed having neighbors. He liked people, even if a lot of them seemed nervous around him. It didn't matter what he would like, however. It was safer this way, for him, and for them.

It also was quieter … usually. Tonight was different, of course. It was October 30th and the wail of sirens had been non-stop since yesterday. The city was burning, just like it did every year, and the cops and the crooks and the kids were all out in full force.

While Hunter was concerned that some dumb teenagers might douse his shop in gasoline, thinking it was abandoned, he mostly didn't mind Devil's Night. Sure, there were bad guys out there burning people out of their homes for insurance money, but mostly he saw the fires as a force for purification. A good chunk of the arsons were started by pissed-off parents razing drug dens and gang clubhouses. He could get behind that.

More importantly, Devil's Night was also a distraction for the unknowing. The police were so busy dealing with the arsons and the gang-related crime, that he could mostly hunt in peace. All the distractions made it easier to slip in, make the kill, and blend back into the crowds of troublemakers and good Samaritans roaming the streets.

The thing that bothered him most about Devil's Night was the noise. Hunter was sick of the cacophony of sirens—fire engines wailing over the chirp of police cruisers and the warble of ambulances. Hunter turned up the volume on the tape deck, blaring Aretha Franklin. He grooved to the gospel music and danced back to the workbench.

"The first rule to killing vampires is to flush all that movie bullshit from your head. You dig, Benny? This ain't some Hammer horror flick."

There was a moment of silence while Hunter gave Benny a chance to respond. Benny stayed silent. Hunter shrugged and continued his lecture.

"Oh no, Benny Boy, these are some flesh-ripping, baby-eating, blood-sucking demons of the pit. We're talking real old-world folklore kinda shit."

Hunter held the knife up and inspected its edge. Unsatisfied, he went back to dragging the blade across the stone. Kind of sharp wasn't good enough. Poor tools lead to sloppy work. Sloppy work would leave you dead or in jail.

"The second rule is having and maintaining the right gear. God only helps those who help themselves, so you hide behind a cross and you'll end up as Vlad chow. As far as stakes go, I've never met a man strong enough to drive one through anybody's heart, let alone a mythic monster. You're better off with a good, sharp knife."

With the knife's edge finally to his liking, Hunter placed it on his workbench and picked up his Tippman SMG 60 paintball gun. He fired three rapid shots at a vaguely human-shaped target painted on the far wall of the garage. All three splattered in the center of the head.

"The paintballs are infused with garlic, and believe it or not, that does actually work. It won't kill them mind you, but it messes them up right good. Blinds 'em a little and burns up their senses."

Benny yawned and laid his head down on the beat-up sofa in the corner of the shop. He closed his eyes and let out a long huffing breath.

"Sorry to bore you, my man," Hunter said, a bit offended, and went about the work of securing all his gear to his person. The Tipman hung from a lanyard over his shoulder. He sheathed the Bowie knife, along with a boot knife as a backup. Finally, he donned a cheap duster that hid his weapons from prying eyes.

"I'll leave the music on for you," Hunter said, switching the tape deck to the AM radio function. Classical music, some piece that Hunter had heard a hundred times but couldn't name if you held a gun to his head, played from the speakers. He turned down the volume and regarded Benny with a stern expression.

"Don't let anyone in, but if some asshole kids try to set the place on fire, run away for Christ's sake. You hear me?"

Benny didn't answer. He never did. This was the nature of their relationship, given that Benny was a golden retriever. Still, Hunter hated always having to carry the conversation.

Hunter slipped out through the back door of the auto shop, and into the night. A gray haze hung over the skyline, its edges highlighted in orange. There were devils about alright—both figurative and literal—but it wasn't their night. No, tonight was a hunter's night.

0

Hunter parked his van at the corner of Harper and Whittier. A group of bikers, all wearing the three-piece patch of the Highwaymen Motorcycle Club, sped past. They howled as they weaved between the slower-moving cars on the road. He didn't much care for the Highwaymen, but they weren't his concern. Their brand of evil was mundane, and his skill set was honed for more exotic prey. Plus, there were forces to deal with outlaw bikers. Cops. Other gangs. Karma.

Most of the mom-and-pop bodegas were shuttered for the night. Those that did stay open ran a high risk of being robbed by crackheads in Halloween masks or raided by groups of punk kids. The downside of staying closed meant a higher risk of someone lighting their shops on fire, but hell, there was insurance for that at least.

Hunter walked a few blocks, past drugged-out death rockers and roving packs of kids in cheap plastic masks. Up ahead was the U-Rock, a music hall that catered to the fans of all sorts of degenerate devil music. Hordes of black-clad, makeup-smeared youths stood outside. They smoked cigarettes and stared listlessly into the starless sky.

There was an alleyway behind the club, a place where the bands would load their gear or go to smoke dope between sets. Hunter turned into the alley, already knowing what he needed to do. He'd scoped the place out weeks in advance, as soon as he heard that Sanguine Sex Cult would be playing there.

To the right side of the filthy alley was a rusted fire escape, climbing past floor after floor of boarded windows. Hunter jumped up and caught hold of an iron ladder rung. He was concerned that the rusted metal might give beneath the weight of his considerable frame, but it held.

He settled in, laying on his belly across the rusted iron, and aimed his paintball gun at the backdoor of the club. When the vampire showed itself, he would be ready.

0

Radu smirked as the groupie hesitated, the razor hovering above her chest. There were plenty of crazy girls who were eager to cut themselves open for

102

him, so many that it was almost passe now. The fear and hesitation in this one excited him. He enjoyed watching her inner struggle as it manifested in trembling hands and shallow breaths—that battle between her desire to please him and her reluctance to shed her own blood.

"I thought you wanted to pay tribute," Radu said, with an ambiguous Eastern European accent lifted from B horror films. "If you're just wasting my time, I can find someone else."

"No!" the groupie cried. "I want this!"

Radu took a drag from his cigarette and exhaled a cloud of smoke. The display was just as deliberate and practiced as his accent—a dramatic piece of theater that he had incorporated into the image and personality he had manufactured for himself.

"Then do it."

The groupie's hands trembled as she sucked in a deep breath. The razor hovered above her porcelain chest. Her face tensed and black eyeshadow eclipsed hazel eyes.

"Give yourself to me," Radu said. Usually, he would whisper that line. A breathy whisper really got these kinds of girls going. Unfortunately, the opening band was starting their set, and the squelch of feedback forced him to raise his voice.

The girl gasped as she dragged the razor down her chest, not hard or deep, but enough to draw blood. Radu watched the crimson liquid creep out from the wound. He felt his manhood twitch. There was something about making these girls hurt themselves for him—convincing them into offering not just their flesh but their very lifeblood to him—that got him harder than any lap dance or vanilla porno ever could.

Radu took the razor from the girl's hand as she opened her eyes. He smiled at her, before licking the side of the blade. She swooned watching his tongue caress the flat of the razor ... watching him take pleasure in her essence.

Radu pushed the groupie into the threadbare velvet upholstery of the backstage couch and pressed his lips against her wound. His dick stiffened further at the coppery taste of her blood and the warm wetness of it against his lips.

Blood had been an acquired taste. The first time he'd fed, the warmth and the flavor had sickened him. It had made him want to vomit. That hadn't mattered. He was a being of his own will and creation, not a slave to instinctual disgust. His look, his demeanor, his sound—these were all things he had curated. He'd had a picture in his head of the coolest fucking rock star in the world and he had become it.

Self-becoming didn't stop with the superficial. He wanted to be more than human. He wanted to be a monster, and not just on the stage or in a music video. Radu was determined to become the real thing. It had taken the blood of countless groupies and years spent praying to the darkest of gods, but he could feel the changes in his body. The sensitivity to sunlight. The energizing rush from the taste of fresh blood. The wide berth that death now gave him. Davey, his drummer insisted it was psychosomatic, but what the hell did he know?

"More?" Radu asked, gazing at her with the hypnotic smolder he had perfected in the mirror over the course of years. No answer came from her lips, but her eyes showed hesitation. He wasn't genuinely concerned with her consent, of course, and that hint of fear within her silence was sweeter than the most enthusiastic yes. Licking his canines, Radu opened a second wound across the girl's chest.

She flinched and let out a sharp cry that was nearly lost beneath the music playing in the club. Radu had not hesitated in opening her flesh as she had. This new wound was deeper than the one the girl had inflicted on herself. The blood flowed more rapidly and ran down her cleavage.

Radu lapped up the trail of blood, following it up her chest and to the wound. He spread the cut apart with two fingers and forced the tip of his tongue inside. The groupie protested and tried to pull away, but Radu grabbed her by the throat and held her firm.

"You gave yourself to me," he said, his lips and chin stained red. "You're mine now."

Tears ran down her face, smearing her thick makeup. Radu laughed and dragged the razor across her skin once more.

0

*Dear God ignite my soul, so that I may be your flaming sword.*

Hunter had been mentally repeating the phrase for hours, his eyes fixed on the backdoor of the club the entire time. It was a simple mantra intended to keep him focused and awake while also protecting his mind from the vampire's will. It had never failed him in any of his hunts.

*Dear God ignite my soul, so that I may be your flaming sword.*

He'd first discovered the power of mantras when he'd served in The Marine Corps, toward the end of Vietnam. By focusing on a simple axiom, repeating it in his mind, he'd been able to keep his wits about him in the hell that was the jungle.

*Dear God ignite my soul, so that I may be your flaming sword.*

It was in 'Nam that he had encountered his first vampire. They were numerous there, more so than in The States. They stalked the jungles there, tracking men by the smell of their blood and materializing from the soil and the shadows. They trapped soldiers in pits and ate them alive as they writhed on punji sticks. But Hunter had learned their ways. He'd turned the tables and became the predator.

*Dear God ignite my soul, so that I may be your flaming sword.*

He'd killed countless monsters in Vietnam. On one occasion he'd helped wipe out an entire village of the undead. The demonic beasts posed as men, women, and children, but he'd seen them for what they were. Not one of them escaped, and he'd been sure to cut out the hearts and sever the heads of every corpse.

*Dear God ignite my soul, so that I may be your flaming sword.*

The rear entrance to the club opened. All thoughts of 'Nam and the horrors he'd experienced evaporated. The only terrors that mattered were the ones in the present. The only monsters he needed to worry about were the ones he had yet to kill.

Radu Caligari, the lead singer of Sanguine Sex Cult, sauntered into the alleyway. His frame was stick-thin, like a walking skeleton and his face was smeared with blood. A lit cigarette dangled from his black-taloned fingers. Hunter couldn't get over the creature's hubris. Most vampires tried to hide from the world. They sought to blend in and hunt from the shadows. Radu flaunted his unholy existence. He spat in the face of man and God alike. The fact that no one else had stepped up to slay the abomination was a sad example of how soft and decadent mankind had become.

There was no changing the state of the world. He couldn't make others turn their back on sin. He couldn't persuade mankind to take up arms against evil. No, he couldn't inspire others to virtue, but God had granted him the skill and the stomach to do what the rest wouldn't.

Hunter set his sights on Radu's face. He held his breath and watched him in the scope for several seconds. The monster's visage sickened him. Its bloody maw and yellow teeth turned his stomach. Its pallid, corpselike complexion made his skin crawl. Its wicked smile cast shadows across his heart.

*Dear God ignite my soul, so that I may be your flaming sword.*

The Tippman was nearly silent. What little sound it made—a soft *pfft*—was lost behind Radu's screams as three garlic-infused paintballs exploded against his face. He stumbled and fell into the wall. His curated accent gave way to the angry curses of a New Yorker as he pawed at his eyes.

Hunter swung himself off the edge of the fire escape and dangled for a moment before releasing his grip. He rolled as he hit the ground, dispersing the force of impact and keeping his momentum. Springing to his feet, Hunter let the paintball gun hang from its lanyard and rushed for his prey.

He charged Radu like a linebacker, driving his shoulder just below the monster's ribs and crushing him against the brick facade of the club. Bones gave, snapping more easily than he'd expected. As flippant as this vampire was with flaunting its dark power, Hunter had expected it to be heartier.

The vampire wheezed. It was trying to speak, but only blood and foul breath passed its lips. All the better, Hunter thought. A silent ghoul couldn't use its words or voice as a weapon. It couldn't exploit one's pity or Christian virtue. It couldn't hypnotize or trick you.

Vampires healed quickly, Hunter knew. Its ribs would pop back into place any minute, and the garlic would only blind the beast for so long. If he was to survive, he needed to press his advantage.

Hunter threw Radu onto the filthy concrete and produced his knife. He fell upon the beast and raised his weapon high into the air. The blade gleamed in the yellow illumination from the streetlights as Hunter plunged his knife into the monster's heart.

Radu stopped moving. He no longer tried to fight or scream. His chest did not rise and fall. Hunter knew he wasn't dead for real, not just yet. The knife through the heart had only paralyzed the vampire. There was still one step. The head would have to be removed.

Hunter muttered his prayer, this time aloud, as he retrieved a cable saw from his pocket. He wrapped the thin bit of wire around Radu's neck like a garrote. He worked the tool back and forth. The flesh put up no resistance, and a torrent of blood gushed forth from Radu's neck. The cartilage and bone were a bit tougher; Hunter sawed through those easily as well.

The stolen lifeblood from countless victims drained from Radu's decapitated corpse. Hunter liked to think that this freed the souls of the vampire's victims and allowed them to move on. He imagined himself holding open the gates of Heaven for them.

Hunter waited and watched until the blood stopped flowing, confident that God would shield him from prying eyes. He'd thought that Radu was a vampire of some advanced age. He'd expected that his body would turn to dust as the ravages of time descended on the undead flesh all at once. Instead, Radu's corpse sat cold and dismembered, still playing at being human … just like all the others he had slain.

"Why won't he turn to dust?" Hunter whispered. "Why don't they ever turn to dust?"

# THE BLACK CLOUD

Pardon me, as I sharpen my knife while introducing the next gory selection. It's always ~~expected~~ important to have your edge honed, for you never know when you might need to use it. The two cousins you're about to meet are rivals in more than just wrestling. Kaleb has ~~been~~ adopted by his aunt Brenda after a house fire which killed his parents.

Scotty, the older cousin, is jealous of the attention his mother gives the boy. When Brenda brings home a scrap of black cloth to fashion into a cloak for Kaleb's birthday, Scotty seeks to eliminate the "dwarfan" in the ring once and for all, but Kaleb, aided by a familiar visitor, will show just how sharp a divide he has cut between mother and son.

# THE BLACK CLOUD

"**R**.I.P!" Kaleb screamed, vaulting off the nylon rope of the homemade wrestling ring. His cloak, fashioned from a faded black bed sheet, lapped the dry desert air, and the early evening sun winked off the silvery metallic coating of his plastic scythe. Scotty, distracted by the sound of his mother's pickup truck rolling up the long driveway, was knocked onto his back on the yellowed mattress at the center of the ring. It took only one deft thrust with Scotty's oversized Mangler gloves for the older cousin to throw the younger one off. If it were any other time Scotty would have instantly retaliated for the cheap affront by pummeling the dwarf-an (a portmanteau Scotty had coined himself—the blending of "dwarf" and "orphan") until he was bloodied and bawling. It was, as the Mangler always said, about *dominance,* and this was Scotty's house after all—not the dwarf-an's.

But today was different. Both of them had been waiting weeks for this, and as Scotty rolled under the rope out of the ring and began running towards the house, Kaleb was quick on his heels, moving as fast as he could in Scotty's two-sizes-too-large hand-me-down sneakers. The boys rounded the side of the house and stood panting in the driveway, shielding their eyes from the rush of dust that accompanied the truck as it rumbled to a stop in front of one of the garage's three bays.

"Did they have it ma? Did you *get it*?"

"Hold on a damn second, will ya Scotty?" his mother said. She was a big woman, her round face slightly rouged from the grocery store excursion, her cottony, pale mane fanning out thinly in the breeze as she opened the door. A freshly lit one-hundred length menthol cigarette dangled from her lips, the smoke from it making her eyes pinch. Her huge breasts swung ponderously as she shimmied out of the truck, doling out plastic sacks to the boys who immediately began to root through them. "Hurry up and get them in the house! Frozen stuff's already half thawed …"

Scotty and Kaleb carried the bags inside, through a breezeway that reeked of mothballs and sneaker odor and into the kitchen where they began tearing through them in earnest, pushing past packs of cellophaned ground beef, beefsteak tomatoes, boxes of snack cakes, macaroni salad, family-sized bags of barbeque potato chips, bacon, white bread, tubs of margarine, a gallon of brown/white/pink ice cream, and other sundries along with the day's newspaper folded over twenty or so scratch-off lottery tickets. Behind them Kaleb heard his Aunt Brenda grunting up the short flight of steps. She emerged in the room just as Scotty was tossing a bag of stuff that didn't contain what he was looking for onto the floor.

"Don't break them eggs!" she shrieked.

In the black bag beside his Uncle Pete's nightly sixer of Old Steed tallboys, Kaleb spotted the plastic tape case. He drew it out with a triumphant roar. A second later Scotty ripped it from his hands and started down the basement stairs.

They spent most of their indoor time in the basement; it was cool and there was a room with a television and a VCR and a bunch of video games. Scotty already had the tape in the player and was flopped down on the old couch in front of the TV. Kaleb sat Indian style on the other end and pulled his black bed sheet cloak around him, his legs flapping up and down in anticipation.

For a long moment there was only black on the screen. Tape hiss. A sound like someone hitting redial on a phone, and then the big UWA (Universal Wrestlers Association) logo in a cut granite font. Black again; then distant cheering in the darkness as the camera swept over the crowd, half of which held coffin-shaped signs with R.I.P.P.E.R. scrawled in white across them. The other half pumped cutouts of giant red fists on sticks. Everyone seemed almost insane with excitement. The camera swooped into the center of the ring where a man in a purple spangled coat and silver hair greased back into a ducktail grabbed a microphone dangling from the rafters and announced Johnny "The Mangler" Mangles. The wrestler appeared at one end of the arena, a mass of peachy muscle with an impeccable blond crew cut, accompanied by a burst of red-white-and-blue fireworks and blaring electric guitar music. He strutted slowly towards the center of the arena, thrusting his huge fists up and down to the chant of his supporters (Scotty joined in now- *MANG-ler, MANG-ler, MANG-ler)* and ducked under one of the elastic bands into the ring. More fireworks went off as he paced around, flexing and posturing and throwing fake punches with his massive fists.

Suddenly the lights went out and the guitar riffs cut, replaced by a darkly chanting chorus. At the opposite end of the arena from which The Mangler had made his entrance a door opened and a low green fog began to creep. A wolf howled; a witch cackled. And then a line of skeletons banging "flesh" drums with femur bones began to march down the long, sloping isle. They circled the ring, their pounding trance-like. Backlit by a blue-silver glow in a doorway high up behind them a shadow figure appeared. Everyone—even The Mangler—turned to regard the hooded figure as it drifted, almost as if floating, through the miasmatic mist towards center stage. When it reached the ring, the figure drew back its hood. The Ripper's bald head was painted white, his skull face neon yellow, the eyes and nose and lips and cheek hollows black. He undid the ties of his cloak and threw it off, revealing a black body suit screen printed like an X-ray.

The two wrestlers approached one another; the Ripper grinning his painted death grin while Johnny Mangles pretended to crack his huge knuckles. The man in the purple spangled coat quickly stepped back, his place taken by a referee who was already trying to keep the men apart as they glared at one another while their respective smoke curled behind them. The Ripper was leaner than the Mangler, the curves of his muscles clearly visible beneath the tight, skeleton-printed nylon uniform. It looked odd, as if he were turned inside out. For a moment Kaleb was too in awe to speak; he just sat there on the smelly old couch, his whole body in frisson under the bed sheet cloak. The bell dinged, the referee scuttled back and out of the way. The championship round was about to begin.

◊

Upstairs, Brenda took three asprin and unpacked the rest of the bags. The headache was bad, and the boys' shouting didn't help. But she couldn't help smiling as she listed to Kaleb. It was the first genuinely kid-like sound he'd made since they'd taken him in. She tried to recall the last time she'd heard him laugh, and decided it was on his previous birthday—exactly one year ago today. The weather had been the same, hot enough to sunstroke the devil, and Pete had been making burgers and dogs on the grill. Somehow a can of hairspray and a lighter became involved. The makeshift blowtorch made Kaleb laugh so hard he'd fallen into the dust in tears. In retrospect Brenda decided it was funny, though at the time it only reminded her of the fireballs she'd seen blasting through the windows of her brother's house three months earlier.

She put away the groceries, leaving the items for the surprise birthday dinner on the counter, then picked up the last bag and carried it to the dining room. Balled on top of a sheet cake in one of the plastic sacks was a huge swathe of black fabric she'd found snagged on a guard rail on the way home. It had been just beyond what had almost certainly been a fatal accident, featuring the charred shell of an overturned sedan and a bus with an accordioned front end that had smashed into the mountain. That was when her headache had began—sitting in the interminable traffic, fretting over Kaleb's birthday ice cream melting and Pete's Old Steeds being warm when he got home. Also, a storm was coming, and she hated driving in the rain. In the west the clouds had been darker than she'd ever seen. There had been one cloud in particular, like a floating plume of soot, hovering on the outskirts of the wreck like a gawker hoping to get a peek at the carnage. *What kind of rain falls from a thing like that?* she'd wondered nervously.

The idea had come to her fully formed the moment she'd seen the fabric. It had been cool to the touch despite hanging in the 101 degree sun at 3pm. It was just as cool now as she spread it out on the dining room table. The black was so opaque it hardly seemed like cloth at all, more like a hole that had opened in the table. Three of the four irregular edges were ragged; the last ended in a neat hem. Brenda lifted one corner, fingering the sable edges, then folded it into thirds and considered it again. Kaleb was small—like his dad had been at his age. She reckoned it would be enough.

Downstairs the noise was intensifying. She wouldn't have much time before the match was over and Pete got home, cranky and demanding his "goddamned dinner."

She poured what remained of the morning's coffee into a stained travel mug, nuked it until boiling, then carried the cup and the cloth down the hall to her sewing room. The chair creaked under her considerable weight as she squatted at the rectangular folding table.

Here, she spread the cloth again, grabbed her tape and measured: four feet by five, with just enough room to fashion a hood. She sipped the black liquid in her cup, pulled a face, then switched on the gooseneck lamp, and held one of the fabric's torn edges under the light. The grimace left by the taste of the bitter coffee turned to a deep frown. Under the hundred-watt bulb, the cloth didn't appear black at all, but brown—brown and very much like freshly-overturned soil. The dirt seemed to be crawling even, a softly undulating mass with something just beneath it, just about to break through.

Brenda dropped the cloth and backed away from the table. Was it fleas? Bed bugs? She stood, opened the curtain to let in some natural light. Reluctantly, she picked it up between two fingers and held it to the window. In the daylight the cloth remained black and innocuous. Brenda held it under the lamp again, but this time saw no movement. She closed her eyes, her temples pulsing. The headaches were bad, but they'd never made her *see* things before.

She switched off the lamp, deciding to work by natural light as she picked up her shears and began evening the rough edges of the cloth until she had a perfect square, humming a hair-metal ballad as she worked. Once trimmed, Brenda swung the length of fabric over the headless torso of her dress mannequin and took up needle and thread. She worked fast; it was a simple garment, no sleeves, no elaborate tucking, and she was thrilled to discover that the cut would be just large enough.

Yet, as she stitched, she couldn't help but wonder whether creating this embodiment of The End for her traumatized nephew was really such a good idea. Perhaps it was wrong to encourage his increasing obsession with death. She had been glad when Scotty introduced Kaleb to the UWA (though often she wondered if it had been so that her only child had someone smaller to beat on), but it also disturbed her how completely Kaleb had (*identified?*) with The Ripper. She supposed it was some subconscious way of dealing with what had happened. She recalled how the firefighters had found him on the stoop of the blazing house, ghost-white and soot-streaked but alive, unlike his mother and father lying upstairs in their charred bed with the flames licking the hollows of their—

She cut the image off before it spread over her mood like black mold. She'd learned an important lesson since her brother's death (from an afternoon talk show, no less): you *have* to follow the joys in life, no matter how small. For her, Joy was Butter Pecan ice cream, dollar scratch-off lotteries, and most of all, her boy. For her husband, six ice-cold pilsners and stock car racing. For Scotty, wrestling. For Kaleb it was

*Death.*

No—she wouldn't let herself settle on that, accurate though she knew it to be. Surely there were other things he loved, and it was her task to find out what they were. One happened to be The Ripper. Well, it was a start. She drew the hood over the mannequin's blank face and continued to sew.

◊

The match was going badly for The Ripper. He'd been pinned three times to Johnny Mangles' one (the last time to an eight count, during which Kaleb thought his thundering heart would explode) and now the carefully painted neon skull mask was little more than a smear of sweaty yellow paste nearly revealing the real man beneath. This, however, turned out to be nothing compared to the look of surrender in Kaleb's hero's eyes when the Mangler got him in a final headlock and began parading him around the ring, grinning in skull parody at the audience. Scotty, sensing victory, started to chant *MANG-ler* along with the frenetic crowd. The Mangler tossed his opponent into the ropes; The Ripper bounced back in Johnny Mangles' direction where the massive fist was extended. As it connected, the yellow paint smeared up one side of The Ripper's face like a wound opened with a blade and he fell to the ground, utterly still. The Mangler pinned him.

*"NOOOO!!"* Kaleb screamed as the referee dropped to the mat on all fours, hammering out the count with his palm.

*One ... Two ... Three ...*

Scotty leapt up and down on the couch, punching the drop ceiling panels with his giant Johnny Mangler fists in time with the count.

*Four ... Five ... Six ...*

The man in the purple spangled coat with the silver ducktail hair waited just outside the ring with the huge golden championship belt, his eyes on the winner-apparent.

*Seven ... Eight ...*

A ripple went through the TV screen; a black bar accompanied by a buzzing noise, distortion, and then the unmistakable sound of VCR eating tape.

*Nine ...*

Kaleb was pleading silently: *No, you* can't *lose. Get up, Get UP! I've got nothing. Please ... nothing ...*

The Ripper, flatlined until that moment, slowly lifted his head. The eyelids opened, the blank pits fixed on Kaleb, and then the picture crinkled, twisted, and the screen turned solid blue.

Scotty vaulted off the couch, bellowing and throwing his foam Mangler fists at the television. He pushed the Eject button on the VCR. The machine groaned as it sluggishly regurgitated the cassette. Black tape, still snagged in the internal mechanism, trailed behind it like intestines. In his panic Scotty yanked too hard trying to free it, and in a sudden inexorable moment the tape snapped. The older cousin held up the wreckage of the rented film in disbelief. And that's when Kaleb suddenly realized: *They never got to ten. The Ripper didn't lose!* He began leaping up and down on the couch himself now, shouting "R.I.P.! R.I.P! R.I—"

Scotty's bare fist, connecting with Kaleb's lips, arrested the last letter. A thin ejecta of blood shot out onto the glass coffee table in front of the couch as the smaller boy fell sideways, smacking his head on the cement floor. A second later his cousin was straddling him, pounding his face and ribs.

*"He LOST! Say it you little shit eating brat, he FUCKING LOST— FUCKING SAY IT!!"*

Between blows Kaleb glimpsed his only defense, and brought his knee up between Scotty's legs. The older boy looked comically stunned as he fell limp into the TV stand. Kaleb scuttled backwards, blood pouring down his face as he scurried towards the stairs, screaming for his aunt.

Ô

The sewing room was directly over the TV in the basement, so Brenda had heard the fight the moment it began. The sound of the first shriek had made her stick herself with the needle, and now she sucked blood from her thumb as she shuffled around the table towards the door. Approaching the basement door, Kaleb all but knocked her over as he emerged up the stairs. Gory, screaming, Kaleb. Scotty, she noticed darkly, hadn't held back, and the first thing she thought was *he's just like his daddy.* Not that she was surprised by what she saw. Scotty had made it clear—many times in many cruel ways—that he had not been happy about Kaleb coming to live with them. It hadn't helped that she had paid more attention to her nephew than her son in those horrid subsequent months after the fire, sleeping beside him during the stretch of nightmares, treating him like her own even as he moaned endlessly about wanting to go home ("home" she knew was the figurative place, not the blackened shell at 561 Archer Rd). It seemed to have cleaved something between her and Scotty, and to some degree between her and Pete, but what was she supposed to do? It had been up to everyone to make an adjustment. She hadn't asked for this anymore than Kaleb, but she was determined to make the best of it because it was the right thing to do—for her brother as much as for Kaleb.

And now as she looked at the boy, at his face slimed with snot and blood, she became furious, and felt the rare urge to let it loose on Scotty. But she wasn't Pete.

She took Kaleb's hand and led him to the bathroom where she washed and dressed the scratches and bruises. The boy had gone weirdly quiet during this, staring distantly, barely wincing as she applied the alcohol. She hoped that she was being as gentle as Kate would have been. Close, she supposed, but never just the same. Kaleb was Kate's pup after all. But Kate was dead, and though Brenda had tried on several occasions to "mother" Kaleb, the boy seemed nevertheless to be drifting further, always further. What she really wanted to say was *I know this has been hard on you, but damn if it hasn't been hard on me too, kid. We're like in our own little lifeboats rowing away from the same shipwreck when we should be in the same one.*

After cleaning him up, she led him back into the kitchen and gave him a little plastic barrel of red drink from the fridge. She was about to send him off to his room (previously Scotty's; now one the boys shared) when she heard, as if he'd read her thoughts, Scotty slam and lock the bedroom door.

"Big K, why don't you go outside and play while I fix supper?" Brenda suggested. The boy looked up at her dully for a moment, one eye beginning to swell, fresh blood beading on his puffy bottom lip, then turned and started toward the back door.

⚰

Kaleb crossed the sun-blasted yard, emptying the red drink into the dry and fissured earth as he walked. He went as far as he could—to the wooden perimeter fence which doubled as the property line—climbed up it, and perched atop one of the wooden rails. His bed sheet cloak was torn at the neck line and hung limply off one shoulder. He slowly undid the knot at his throat and let the wind carry it off, a flailing bat skittering along the rocky terrain. He sat staring at the leather-colored mountains standing like cairns over the graves of giants on the vast desert plain. The sky was a swirl of yellow and orange against a backdrop of deepening blue. The colors made him miss his mother and father though he wasn't sure why. It was his birthday today—he was finally double digits—and he wondered if anyone knew, and even if they did, if they cared. He supposed his aunt might. She was nice enough, though her affection always seemed forced—a duty. Still, she was much nicer than Uncle Pete, who never spoke to him and looked at Kaleb as if he were a desert rat skittering through the house; and Scotty, who Kaleb was now seriously beginning to believe might actually kill him before he reached eleven.

He looked back at the house—a sagging tin-sided modular adrift on an ocean of baked earth and sandstone bergs. White sheets and faded, threadbare towels and Uncle Pete's underwear hung from a line run from the garage soffit to one of the wrestling ring poles. It was all so different from the steel and glass townhouse in the city suburb, with its potted monsteras and green lawns and automatic sprinklers. Why had it happened the way it did? Why had he smelled the smoke when his parents hadn't? Why had he survived—only to live *here*?

He turned away, wiping his eyes with the back of his hand, and looked again at the ragged skyline of rock. Drifting in his direction across the wash of sunset colors was a single black stratocumulus. It moved between two serrated mountain peaks a few hundred yards ahead of him, and there seemed to pause. Head tilted, Kaleb stared at it, recognizing the specific opacity, the shade of the char-black. He thought he could smell it too—a musk like scorched, wet wood drifting on the desiccated wind.

0

When he got back to the house Kaleb found it a place transformed. A generic banner reading "Happy Birthday" in shiny colored letters spanned the arched doorway between the living and dining rooms. Beyond there were yellow balloons taped to the backs of the chairs and black crêpe paper streamers—Ripper colors—dangling from the ceiling fan. On the table was a sheet cake with his name on it, and on either side, two paper bags which most likely contained presents. There was a mixing bowl full of potato chips and a tub of macaroni salad with a spoon sticking out of it and corn on the cob stacked like logs. The table was set for four; Kaleb's place was marked by the plastic scythe hanging by its blade over the back of the chair opposite where Uncle Pete sat.

Brenda walked into the room carrying a sack of sandwich buns in one hand and a plate of sliced onions and lettuce and tomatoes in the other. The kid's unfiltered surprise made her grin. She set the stuff on the table looked at Kaleb with her hands on her hips.

"What, did ya think I'd forget?"

She'd hoped for a smile, perhaps even a listless 'thank you'. She did not expect the sudden emotion, the sudden embrace. At the same moment Scotty appeared in the doorway leading from the kitchen with a platter of grilled hamburgers. He gave them a dead sort of glare as he tossed the plate of meat onto the table and walked back out.

They ate the birthday feast in silence, while the wind threw sand and bits of stone at the windows. At some point Uncle Pete gave one of his slow sidelong glances at the sliding glass doors and said: "Sky's blacker than a steer's asshole. Better bring them sheets in."

"We just had rain last week," Brenda said, picking corn from her teeth with a plastic fork tine. "I bet it'll pass over."

"Pass over hell ..." Pete muttered. He downed the last sip from his Old Steed tallboy as he rose and started toward the kitchen.

"Ain't you havin' cake with us?" Brenda called after him. From the other room came a distant belch, the sound of a can crunching and another opening, and finally the TV clicking on in the living room. Brenda turned back at the boys with a look of resigned dismay.

"Go on and open your stuff big K," she said.

Scotty, arms crossed, glowered from his chair as Kaleb grabbed the first of the two bags. It contained a dog-eared coloring book of big rigs, half of which had already been colored-in. Most likely it had been Scotty's—maybe even a gift on *his* tenth birthday. "That one's from your Uncle Pete," said his aunt. She slid the second bag toward him. It was much larger than the first, the contents bulging the sides. "This one's from me."

Kaleb looked in the bag; there appeared to be nothing inside, just black.

"Go on, take it out," she prodded.

*Take what out?* Kaleb thought as he reached in the bag, as he felt his fingers connect with something plush and coarse and quite cold. Startled, he drew his hand quickly, ripping the bag in the process. Black fabric spilled out like oil onto his lap. It seemed to be some sort of coat. He held the garment up, frowning at first. Then his mouth fell open as he began to understand what it was. His eyes moved from the cloak to his aunt and then back again. In his periphery he saw Scotty staring incredulously, brows pinched. Kaleb stood with the heavy thing in his hands, letting the paper bag slide off his lap and fall to the floor like molted skin. He swung the cloak around his shoulders; it made a profound *whoosh* as it swept around him and settled ponderously onto his slight frame—a perfect fit. Brenda watched all of this, biting her bottom lip with her crooked front teeth, trying to suppress her grin so that Scotty wouldn't see. "Pull the hood up," she said. Kaleb did as she asked. The fabric seemed to creep and writhe along his flesh; a strange sensation, but not an unpleasant one.

After the brief gift unwrapping, Brenda cleared the disposable dinner plates and returned with a pack of candles and matches. It didn't occur to her that Kaleb might not want to see the little flames until after she'd lit them and slid the cake in front of him. But Kaleb didn't seem bothered. He gazed levelly at the many small fires from under the hood, gazed so long the wax began to drip on the frosting. His face hovered still and pale as a waning gibbous moon.

"Well go on then and make your wish before them candles melt!" Brenda chuckled uneasily.

Kaleb looked up at Scotty. His wish was a single word which the older boy seemed to intuit; he nodded as it passed between them silently—*rematch*—as Kaleb blew out the candles.

⚰

Fifteen minutes later the boys stood at the center of the ring made of broomsticks and nylon rope and the old mattress Scotty had been conceived on twelve years earlier. Scotty hadn't brought the Mangler gloves. No, he wanted to feel his bare fists connecting with the dwarf-an's face; he wanted to see the kid's blood and snot squirt out of his face. And he wouldn't quit there. He'd keep on beating him until the little fucker wasn't moving anymore, and then he would wipe his own ass with that cloak and piss on it and maybe do that other thing—that nasty new thing he'd discovered recently—all over it. Yes, he'd do *that* too, and then he'd run away from this middle-of-nowhere shitbox that reeked of his dad's beer farts and his mother's sadness and maybe he would hitchhike to the UWA headquarters where he could sweep floors or polish The Mangler's trophies or maybe even become a Mangler himself. *Skull Crusher Scott.* Yeah, that sounded pretty fuckin' rad.

Scotty heard footsteps approaching the ring. He turned and saw the dwarf-an standing a yard or so from him in the ring, head bent, face hidden beneath the hood of the cloak. The boy moved as if floating, climbed under the rope and took his place diagonally across from Scotty.

"You should have died in that fire," Scotty said. He thought this would've made the kid attack, but Kaleb didn't move. He just stood staring silently down at the mattress. "She's *my* mother, you know. She'll never *love* you. You'll never be part of this family. Do you hear me shit stain? I said you should be dead." The sky rumbled, the clouds moving swift and low in the rising wind. Scotty screamed: "*I wish you were fucking dead!*" and took two big steps forward, teeth bared. Kaleb looked up. There was one eternal moment during which Scotty processed what he was seeing—no yellow paint, no plastic Ripper's Halloween mask, only the white of sun-bleached bone. And then the rain came.

0

Brenda congratulated herself as she knotted the plastic ties on a full-to-bursting bag of kitchen trash. She decided she was even more proud of the cloak than her Freedom Quilt, now on permanent display behind Plexiglas in town hall. Maybe it was time to think about making a little business out of her hobby, make some of her *own* money. *Yes*, she thought. And Pete wouldn't have to know anything about it. She pondered this, considering the logo for her business cards as she shuffled across the kitchen with the bag in the direction of the back door. She opened it, stepped outside and tossed the sack in the bin and then started toward the sheets, whipping and snapping in the high wind. The wind was hot, like the heat radiating up from the baked earth under her feet, but the rain was cold and sharp. She unpinned the first sheet, hurrying on to the next. She didn't see the boys until the second sheet was down. It was not raining in the ring; a large shape hovered above it, a simultaneous object and void. For a moment she didn't understand what they were doing out there. Then she saw Scotty's expression. This time it would be sutures for Kaleb, maybe worse.

She dropped the sheets, screaming not her son's name but Pete's. The rain began to fall harder, an unremitting torrent pelting her and ricocheting around her off the parched ground. It happened in the ten steps it took her to reach the ring. Through the deluge Brenda saw Scotty glance at her, hold her gaze an instant, and then attack. Kaleb raised his arms, parting the cloak. Up came the UWA Ripper scythe, the blade gleaming like satin in the muted lightning threading the clouds. It swung, cutting the air with a hiss, a lethal pendulum arcing upward and catching Scotty just under the lower left rib, passing cleanly through his right shoulder. A spray of blood shot out like a lawn sprinkler, reddening the mattress, a momentary warm misting on the air. The hovering mass/void began to distend, a shadow forming into a gaunt and ossified hand as it descended towards Kaleb. The boy dropped the sickle and reached upwards, a shred of like color reintegrated from whence it had been torn. The claw closed around him and then retracted skyward like a dissipating tornado.

Brenda flopped into the ring, hair hanging like thread. She gathered the upper portion of her son into her lap. There was a moment of understanding, of knowing before her sanity yawed and departed with the fading rain. She thought: *I can put him back together.* That was her job in this family—to bind together what always seemed to want to come undone.

She turned his head toward her.

"Momma's gonna fix this, Scotty."

Scotty's eyes were on the blade, its peeling silver plastic coating glinting in fading flashes of cloud-drown lightning.

# DESTROYED BY SUPERNOVA

Death is big business and there are opportunities aplenty for the savvy entrepeneur. Some make their money putting folks in boxes. I make mine crafting those boxes. But what if there were a device that could predict the nature of your death?

Would you press that button and discover what form the reaper will take for you? In hopes to cheat death, our friend Eli does just that, but there are some things you just can't run away from.

# DESTROYED BY SUPERNOVA

**"T**his is it."

Seth stopped halfway down the alley, in front of an ancient, rusted door set into a crumbling brick wall. The building appeared derelict. A fire escape that looked to be more rust than iron led up to boarded-over windows on all three levels. Eli wasn't an architecture buff, but he couldn't imagine that the place was younger than a few centuries.

Eli took a deep breath and immediately regretted it. He was assaulted by a mixture of piss and warm trash, mingling with the scent of steak and fries from the barbecue joint around the corner.

"This?" Eli replied. He didn't believe that this crumbling old building could contain the technological marvel he had been promised. Something so revolutionary had to be held in a well-funded lab or on the campus of some big tech school. Then again, Microsoft had started in a garage, so perhaps it wasn't such a far-fetched idea.

"I know it doesn't look like much, but this machine was built by one guy, not some corporation. Once it goes public it's gonna change everything! We're talking some event horizon shit!" Seth was overwhelmed with excitement as he spoke.

"Forgive my skepticism."

Normally Eli was the furthest thing from a skeptic. His life had been spent chasing dreams and fairy tales, as well as rank and membership in fantastical cults and crackpot organizations. At various points in his life, Eli had identified as a Thelemite, a Scientologist, a chaos magician, and a neo-Lemurian. None of those paths had brought tangible improvement to his life, so more recently Eli had turned to science.

These days he considered himself a transhumanist– an individual who believes in cultivating science toward the goal of creating stronger, smarter, and virtually immortal human beings. Gene therapy, bio-hacking, cybernetic augmentation—basically any science that *Joe Average* might find unpalatable or ethically questionable was of interest to the transhumanist movement.

The one thing that Eli's ever-shifting worldview seemed to gravitate around was an overwhelming fear of death. From reincarnation to technology-driven apotheosis, each of Eli's revolving beliefs was reached not by logic but by an inability to reckon with the idea of oblivion. The thought of simply not being was too much for him.

A tarnished doorbell hung from red and white wires poking out of the brick. Seth pressed his finger to the button and a harsh buzzing noise could be heard from behind the door. After a few seconds, a slightly softer buzz responded, signaling that the door was now unlocked.

"This is history in the making, Eli! And we're at the ground level, man!"

"That remains to be seen," Eli spoke the words with a practiced detachment.

The aesthetic inside the building was in step with the exterior. A narrow hallway with brick walls and a floor to match stretched out in front of Eli and Seth. Above them was a plaster ceiling, dotted with yellow-brown water stains and blisters of peeling paint. A rusted, cast-iron staircase awaited them at the end of the hallway.

They paused at the stairs, which looked only a bit more stable than the fire escape outside. Seth nudged the first step with his foot and the whole staircase wobbled.

"We might not even live to see this machine of yours, Seth. I can tell you right now how we're gonna die—these stairs."

"It's fine. The dude who built this thing probably goes up and down these steps every day."

Seth led the way downstairs. The steps wobbled with each footfall, causing flakes of rust to rain down beneath them. Eli gripped the handrail, then recoiled his hand at the touch of rust and the sharp edges of chipping paint. Thoughts of tetanus and infection populated his mind and his stomach churned with anxiety.

The staircase terminated two floors down. In the center of the small, dim room before them, an odd machine sat on display. The device, which was crafted from weathered brass and patinated copper, looked vaguely like a keyless version of an antique typewriter. In the center, where one might expect a keyboard should go, there was a single divot. Coming out from the back of the machine were two glass tubes, each containing small coils of wire. The exotic, anachronistic look of the device was all it took for Eli to cast aside his skepticism. His innate thirst for the fantastic was stronger than his cultivated cynicism.

"A bit more H.G. Wells than I was expecting," Seth muttered.

Eli approached the machine, taking time to appreciate the craftsmanship and aesthetic. It looked more like a lovingly crafted movie prop than a functional piece of technology. For Eli, this added a strange sense of legitimacy to the device.

"If you're going to build a machine that can predict your death, you might as well do it with style," Eli said.

Both men jumped as the sound of feedback cut through the air. A deep voice rumbled from speakers in either corner of the room.

"Please, place your finger on the machine."

Seth gestured toward the machine. "Age before beauty, man."

Eli approached the device. Pausing for a moment he considered the possibility that this could be the real deal. If so, this machine could be used by the wise and clever to defeat death. The dim and uninspired, on the other hand, would surely obsess over their mortal ends, unable or unwilling to devise a means of escape. What was promised was equal parts Holy Grail and Pandora's box, all dependent on the scope of the user's vision.

Eli placed his index finger into the divot. The coils sparked to life, and he felt a sharp pain in his finger. Seconds later the typebars furiously hammered a message on a thin strip of paper that was being fed across from somewhere within the machine. When the message was finished the strip of paper was fed out through the right-hand side of the machine and an automated blade cut it free.

"Destroyed by Supernova."

That was the entirety of the message.

〇

Eli rolled out of bed, leaving the hooker from the night before to sleep off her cocaine crash. He'd never slept with a prostitute before, but he'd been doing a lot of things he never had. The knowledge of how he would die didn't cure Eli of his fear of death, but it certainly had helped with his fear of living.

He'd been an anxious mess his whole life, always second-guessing himself and being paralyzed by risk. Every decision was life or death. In the past few months, he'd learned to put happiness over safety, since his safety was guaranteed. He'd driven faster, eaten richer, and fucked with passion and abandon. Never had he lived so fully.

While death was not an immediate concern for him, Eli didn't believe in resting on his laurels, so to speak. He believed that providence was a lazy mistress who often needed a nudge. Thus, Eli scoured the whole of human knowledge, hunting for that discovery that would see him through the millennia ahead.

He moved to the living room, where he sat on the coffee-stained, hand-me-down couch in his apartment, surfing the net on his tablet while the television supplied white noise in the background. This night, like most others, he was scouring the web for any breakthroughs regarding cryogenics, cloning, or stem cell research—basically, anything that could help realize the prediction of his nigh-immortality.

An advertisement for The Oracle™ played on the television. Eli redirected his gaze to the screen. The device had gone public eight months after Eli and Seth took part in the sketchy basement beta test. Seth had been right. It changed everything.

Amazingly, the machines weren't just a novelty. They worked, with astounding accuracy. News stories about celebrity deaths nearly always included a snapshot of their Oracle printout, and it always matched up with what happened.

Not everyone was happy about The Oracle™. Some people still thought it was a scam. Suicide prevention groups were saying that it drove up the number of self-inflicted deaths by telling the mentally ill they were doomed to take their own lives. Others found it to be a gross invasion of privacy and there were even allegations of black magic from certain religious organizations.

None of that stopped the popularity of the new device. Single-use death prediction machines were available in drugstores and at mega-retailers. Reusable, medical-grade versions of the machines were shipping to hospitals around the world. The packaging, to Eli's disappointment, had been greatly altered. Its class and style had been sacrificed for mass-market appeal. The typebars were ousted in favor of a laser printer and the retro, metal body had been replaced with a plastic shell that resembled a video game console.

As the commercial played, depicting all-too-pretty people learning how they would die, Eli couldn't help but think of Seth. Poor Seth. A few weeks after the machine had spit out a paper warning that he'd be "Crushed by a Taurus", Seth expired in an embarrassingly one-sided barroom brawl. Alcohol had gotten the better of him, and he tried to impress a young physics co-ed by mocking the crucifix that a rather large and devout amateur boxer was wearing. The god-fearing fighter, as it turned out, had a birthday of May 1st.

The commercial ended with an attractive couple skydiving while holding hands. Eli was struck by the unnaturally white smiles that came across their faces as they entrusted themselves to gravity. The camera panned out to show the couple's free fall and a voice chimed in over the music. Eli mouthed the words along with it.

"The Oracle—Make fear a thing of the past! "

A more mundane commercial followed, and Eli turned his attention back to the internet. The prediction of his death, *Destroyed by Supernova*, had inspired a renewed vigor in Eli. Not only was the idea of being consumed by an exploding star a grand and romantic notion to him, but it also implied an incredible lifespan. Seeing as Earth's sun is roughly ten times too small to ever go supernova, for the machine's prediction to be true Eli would have to live to see interstellar travel.

Eli was okay with all of these implications. Even the death part if it was to follow such a long and adventurous life. It was Eli's firm belief, however, that providence was a lazy mistress who often needed a nudge. Thus, Eli scoured the whole of human knowledge, hunting for that discovery that would see him through the millennia ahead. On this particular night, he believed he found it.

An article in the latest issue of *New Human*, a transhumanist online magazine, opened with the line *Revolutionary technology promises release from the bonds of entropy and flesh.* The story detailed the unorthodox experiments of an American neurosurgeon named Gary Brentworth. Brentworth had expatriated to South Korea to escape the dogmatic confines that the American government forced scientists to work within.

Eli's heart raced as he read through the rest of the article. Brentworth's work was based around the electronic mapping of neural pathways. The theory was that once the brain was mapped out and chemical levels were examined and recorded, the true core of a person's being could be saved as information and reinstalled on a cloned brain. Brentworth likened the theoretical process for uploading the mapped-out consciousness to the methodology used in creating gramophone recordings. You simply etch the information into the gray matter.

Brentworth's email contact info wasn't listed in the article, but Eli searched the internet until he was able to find it. He brought up two new tabs in his browser. In one he opened his email to send a letter of inquiry to Dr. Brentworth. In the other, he searched flights to South Korea.

0

Dr. Brentworth's laboratory was like nothing Eli had ever seen. The space was filled with technology he couldn't begin to guess the purpose of. Several computers sat in a neat line across a long metal table and tied into monitors lining one wall. While the lab was cramped, it managed to maintain a sterile, hospital-like environment. The whole thing left Eli feeling a bit humbled. While he considered himself a man of science, he was truthfully little more than an armchair technophile.

A woman in a lab coat and surgical mask led Eli to a stainless-steel surgical chair in the center of the room. Eli was reminded of House MD and every brain surgery gone wrong on the show replayed in his mind. He pushed the negative visuals from his thoughts. That was just fiction.

An IV rack with two bags hung beside the chair. One looked like apple juice, the other was crystal clear. Eli tried to read the labels on the bags, but they were written in Korean.

Rubber restraints, the sickly, translucent yellow of surgical tubing, hung loosely from arms and at the base of the stirrups. Beside the chair was a cart holding a tablet, a stainless-steel drill, and several electrodes. Eli eyed the drill and electrodes nervously but assured himself that fate would protect him from death at the hands of such crude tools.

"Please, have a seat."

The young lab assistant spoke perfect English, with only the hint of an accent. Eli once again felt a twinge of insecurity. He nodded and did as she asked, all the while trying not to appear too far out of his depth. He eased down and squinted at the glare of the floodlights pointing down at him.

After a moment Eli heard a voice, distinctly American, with a hint of Texas drawl.

"Hello, Eli. I can't begin to express my gratitude for your boldness."

The white haze of the floodlights was eclipsed by the form of a man dressed in surgical attire. His voice inferred pleasantness but the fact that his expression was hidden under a surgical mask unnerved Eli.

"What we do here today will ring in a new era of mankind, my friend."

Dr. Brentworth's words reminded him of Seth on the night they encountered The Oracle™ prototype. If only Seth was around to see this— a true evolutionary step toward godhood.

"This might be a little tight, but it's for your safety."

The lab assistant tightened the rubber restraints around his limbs. The rubber tugged at his arm and leg hair. A moment later he felt a pinch in his arm, right at the soft point opposite the elbow. Whatever was in the IV felt cold entering his body and elicited a shiver.

"I'm giving you a narcotic painkiller and a paralytic. Unfortunately, I can't sedate you, or else the mapping process won't work. You shouldn't feel any pain, but the noise and the smell might be...unnerving."

"That's fine," Eli nodded. "Let's make history, Doc."

It took a few minutes for the drugs to kick in. The lab assistant clamped Eli's head down in a metal halo and drew several vials of blood from him, while Dr. Brentworth ran through some of the more technical aspects of the procedure. He explained the process for retrieving the data from Eli's mind, what tools and chemicals were needed for encoding the new brain, which he promised had been ethically cloned without a host and farmed without harming anyone.

After checking Eli's vitals and making sure the narcotics and paralytic had taken effect, Brentworth started the drill. Eli felt a slight pressure against the side of his skull. Brentworth was right about the smell and the noise. The experience reminded him of getting a tooth drilled—it was that same putrid, burning odor. As the drill bored into his skull, Eli pondered how the doctor would know where to stop. If his death were not written in the stars, he might have been worried.

Brentworth made a total of four holes in Eli's skull. Each hole had taken an excruciatingly long time. The slow drilling, Eli assumed, was to ensure that his skull didn't crack and to keep the bit from plunging into his brain. He tried to ask Brentworth, just for clarity's sake but the paralytic had robbed him of speech.

"Don't you worry. We're done with most of the nastiness. The holes are drilled and the probes are attached to your brain. You probably didn't even notice the probes."

It was true. Until Brentworth had told him, Eli had no idea that needle-like electrodes were penetrating his gray matter.

"Now we map out your soul, so to speak. An electrical current will travel your neural pathways and record the very essence of who you are." Brentworth's voice shook with excitement.

"Ara, initiate the Supernova software."

Eli's blood turned to ice water at the doctor's words. He willed his hands to move or his feet to kick, but the drugs had frozen his body in place. He tried to scream for them to stop, but his mouth wouldn't move.

# ENDS MEAT

We all have to earn our bread. Mine's made by measuring head to toe, selecting silk and satin, working with plane and plank. Others, like our young friends in this dark vignette, are left to filch — or flay — whatever they can in order to eat.

The brisk "confession" that follows details a girl's reasons for making a rather grisly decision in order to save her starving brother and herself. Abandoned by their alcoholic mother, little Robin must assume the role of mother bird, and do what must be done in order to make "ends "meat."

# ENDS MEAT

**M**y name is Robin Henley. Miss Davis told me that I have nice pen-man-ship. And Mr. DeCait told me that I write well for a girl about to go into fifth grade, better than my class-maits. So I am going to write down what happened instead of tell Mrs. Peterson like you want me to. Because I write better than I talk, and because what happened is not my fault, and if I try to talk about it, espeshally about Denni, I would just start to cry and my father always used to say that crying lets on that you feel things, and that no one should _ever_ be able to know what your felling.

Mother brought Bill Hamm home one night a few days before Christmas. I had popped popcorn and Denni and I were stringing the pieces together with a needle and thred to make some decoration for the tree. It was the last food in the cabinat cause Mother wasnt making any money since she qwit her job at the restarant. The tree was a branch from a pine tree in the park. I found a couple flat sticks in one of the bins in the basement storage place in our building and nailed them together like a cross then nailed this to the bottom of the branch. I put it in the window. We didnt have lights but I thought the popcorn would make it look brighter; we made a popcorn chain in school thats where I learned how to do it. Denni kept poking his finger with the needle and was almost crying. He is only 8. I'm 11 but I'm going to be 12 at the end of this year. Denni kept eating the popcorn because we didnt have any dinner, so I popped it all so we would have something to eat while we were making the decoration. It made a lot and that was good cause we were really hungry.

Bill Hamm was kind of a fat guy and was wearing a white shirt with buttons and a tie and black pants when he came in the door with Mother. He smelled like cigars and like Mothers alkohol. He smelled like something else to kind of sweet, like grass seed that I smelled once in the park. Mother was very drunk and laughing. She met him at the beer joint like the others probabbly. He looked surprised to see me and Denni and said so to my Mother and she looked at us like she usually did and pulled Bill Hamm by his tie toward her bedroom and shut the door. They were laughing in there and drinking more alkohol I think. Then she started making those noises that Denni doesnt understand and I didnt used to understand but do now. They embarrass me now, and make Denni feel funny to I can tell even though he doesnt know whats going on. I learned about all that from Anna Rollins, and ever since then I keep away from boys, afraid that they are going to try and do that to me. I'm not pretty anyway Mark Shovel says. He says that my face looks like a Pilgrm in our history book, and my hair too. My hair is brown and my eyes are brown and my hair is in one braid down my back and I guess I wear plane close like the Pilgrms. All my dresses are brown, but my favorite color is orange and I like to wear orange things when I can ask for them for Christmas like a ribbon or a necklace. Mother gets all our close at the church rummage sale. Denni has a lot of teeshirts that are too big for him and his coat is one that my daddy had when he was a little boy like Denni.

That night when Bill Hamm first came over Denni was so hungry and when we were done with the popcorn decoration we put it on the

tree and looked at it and it was pretty but we were hungry so I took
it down and gave it to Denni. And he ate it, but was still hungry. I
remember that it snowed that night. He got grouchy he was so hungry
and I was hungry too but didnt cry like he started to because I didnt
want him to feel worse and I new he would be scared. So I hugged him
on the couch and he stopped crying soon and we watched the snow and
then Bill Hamm came out of the bedroom and he wasnt wearing any
pants or underwar. He was looking at me funny, and Denni was asleep
and I wish he was awake cause I didnt like how Bill Hamm was looking
at me like he was going to do something bad to me. I was scarred of
him, but there was some smell he smelled like that made me hungry. It
was a wierd felling. He started walking towards me really wobbly, and
I got scarred and woke up Denni and he was really grouchy then and
started to cry. That made Bill Hamm stop and then he walked back to
the bedroom and a few minits after that he left and I locked the door
and put a chair in front of it. Then I went down the hall and looked
at Mother and she was naked like usuall and I put the blanket on her
but she didnt wake up because she had drank so much alkohol. I went
back to the couch and layed with Denni and he fell asleep again but I
couldnt. That smell from Bill Hamm made me so hungry and I wanted
to have something to eat but there was nothing in the cabinet or in the
fridge so I fell asleep.

On the way to school the next day I stoll some donuts from the guy
on East 109th street and put two in Dennis backpack and one in mine. I
tried to be a good student that day but I was so hungry and my stomack
kept making sounds like a car trying to start and the kids made fun of
me. I told Mark that I was goin to stab him in the hand with my pensil
and he told Mr. DeCait and I got sent to the principals office. Mr.
Rigel, hes the principal, told me that I shouldnt thretten anyone and if
I did again hed tell Mother. I wasnt scarred because Mother wouldnt
even care anyway. There were some choclates on Mr. Rigels desk and
when he was talking to Mrs. Aimly the sekratary I took a bunch and

gave them to Denni. He was so happy and smiled a lot and we ate them on the way home from school and it made me happy. Dennis so skinny. Sometimes he gets sick from bein so skinny and gets a bad coff.

That night Bill Hamm came back again. I was doing my multiplication homework and Denni was playing with his cars on the window sill. Mother wasnt laughing this time when they came in, in fact she looked like she had been upset and when she looked at us she looked kinda scarred I thought. Bill Hamm pushed her toward the bedroom and when he shut the door they started talking and Mother had a scarred sounding voice. Then Bill Hamm yelled something and I think he hit her cause Mother screemed and then she was showting and Bill Hamm was showting and he sounded really really mean and scarry. Denni let his cars fall on the floor and hid under the couch and I couldnt get him out for a long time. Mother was crying I think and screeming and there was a lot of baning against the wall over and over. I wanted to hide to but I decided to be brave because I was scarred for my Mother so I got the nife out, the one daddy gave me to keep in my pocket when I walked to school, and went to the bedroom and opened the door a little. Bill Hamm was on Mother and she looked like she was asleep. He was doing that thing that Anna Rollins told me about, doing it to Mother and she had blood coming out of her mouth. I was so scarred to see her like that, but then I smelled that sweet smell and I got hungry. It was Bill Hamm that smelled like that, remember? And I forgot about the nife and prottekting Mother because I just wanted to smell that smell that made me hungry but kinda full and so I watched Bill Hamm and I wished that I could go near him and I wished, this will sound wierd, but I wished that I could <u>bite</u> him. And I started to cry cause I was so hungry and Bill Hamm herd me and then he saw the nife and got real still. He even looked kinda scarred I thought! I looked at him and he looked at me for a long time and then I shut the door because that smell was making me so hungry and I couldnt do nothing about it so I didnt want to feel so hungry anymore.

I thought he would come out and hurt me or hurt Denni because he saw the nife but he didnt come out for the rest of the night. He must have left when me and Denni were asleep because in the morning I got up to go to the bathroom and I saw Mothers door was open and he was gone, but that <u>smell</u> was still in the room. After I peed I got a washcloth and got it wet in the sink and wiped the blood off Mother. She woke up and looked like she didnt know what was going on. Then she started to cry and hugged me real hard and she made me lay down with her and cried a lot more. When she was asleep again I got up because I had to wake up Denni and then we had to get ready for school.

I couldnt steel anymore donuts that day because I almost got cawt by the seller and we had to runaway fast and that made us mor hungry all day. Denni was crying a lot and I felt really bad and started to cry to during class because I new my brother was so hungry and sad. I got sent to the conseller to talk about why I was crying but I wouldnt talk about it and she didnt have any choklats.

It was a hard walk home that day because Denni was so hungry that he kept falling and I had to kinda carry him for the last blocks to the building and up the stairs to the fifth floor where we live. Mother was not home, but she never is when we get home from school, and the house smelled really bad, but it also smelled kind of like Bill Hamm just a little. I was so hungry that I felt kind of crazy I gess you could say. I thought maybe I could go to the park and find something there for me and Denni to eat. Some berries or leaves or something or maybe some mushrooms but I know that they can be poisoness so I didnt want to do that. I didnt want berries or mushrooms anyway I wanted <u>meat</u>. Like a hamburg or something like my daddy would make on the grill on the fire escape before he got killed by that man. The Bill Hamm smell was like meat, but it was like grass too, like I said like grass seed and made me thirsty to. When I ate those hamburgs from the grill they would be full of juice and blood to I gess and I was so hungry when I thought about them and when I think about them now. The blood tasted good but I never told anybody that because it sounded wierd to say that. I really did feel crazy and Denni made me mad because he wouldnt stop crying so I yelled at him and then I felt bad because it wasnt his fault that he was so hungry, hes just a little kid.

Mother didnt come home that night at the time she usually did, or even latter, and I new something was bad then, something bad happened to her like daddy maybe. Denni was real quiet, I think because we had no food and he had no energy to be upset even tho I could tell he was scarred that Mother wasn't home. When Mother wasnt home by 8 I went in her room to see if I could find any money to use to go by me and Denni some food but there was only a few pennys and I new that you cant by nothing with those in this city. But I went back into the living room and told Denni I had found some money and that I was going to by us some food tomorrow and he got real happy. I felt bad about lying to him but I had to cause he was in bad shape, so cold and grouchy before I lied to him. We sat and looked at the tree and we were ok cause it was nice to think about Christmas and about having food tomorrow. I thought about this and pretended even tho I new I'd made up the lie, just so I could feel happyer to like Denni.

Now I have to write down what happened to Bill Hamm. It wasnt my fault what happened to him! I had to take care of Denni and I had to take care of me to so thats why its not my fault!

Bill Hamm opened the door of our appartment that night really slow and looked at me. Denni was asleep on my lap and I didnt move at first because I didnt want him to wake up. Bill Hamm was kind of messy and looked like he had been fighting. I didnt think about Mother, not then because I didnt know that he had just killed her but it makes sense now. He wasnt moving just looking at me and I gess I knew what he wanted. That smell came in the appartment with him and I knew what I wanted to. I got a really good idea. My moth was wattering! I was so hungry, very hungry! So I got up real slow so that Denni didnt wake up and I went to Bill Hamm and grabbed his tie like I saw Mother do. He had been smiling at me kind of strang and then when I did that with the tie his face changed and he looked suprised. "Not here," I said to him and looked back at Denni and he nodded his head like he understood.

I took him down stairs to the basement and turned on the big light. The light is bright in the hallway between the cages with everybodys stuff but the cages are dark. I went to ours and turned the lock to all the numbers and then opened the cage door. Mostly its just daddys stuff in there. Sometimes I would come down to look at it and sit with it and it smelled like daddy and it made me feel like I was sitting with him. It is nice when I am lonely. Bill Hamm followed me and took off his jacket. I layed down next to daddys suitcase and I kept my hand in my pocket and Bill Hamm didnt notice this. He got on top of me then and started doing stuff but I didnt let him do anything like he did to Mother. That smell like grass and salt and water that made me so hungry was so strong I just smelled it and smelled it real deep. Bill Hamm started to say bad things, like I heard him say to Mother when he was in the bedroom with her. I got out my nife and held it out for a minit to make sure I was holding it in a right place by his neck and then I stabbed him real, real hard. All the blood that came out was a suprise. It went all over me and my face and some on my moth. I was grossd out by it at first, but then I tasted some and it tasted really good so I licked it and then licked mor from the place in his neck where it was coming out. Bill Hamm stopped moving after a minit and I got out from under him and I was so hungry then! So I cut some peeces from him, it took a while but I got a lot of good chuncks and took them upstairs to the appartment and put new close on so Denni wouldnt get scarred and then I cooked the Bill Hamm meat in a pan. Denni woke up and his face looked like it was Christmas when he smelled and saw the meat! Then I gave him some and he was so happy to eat it made me so happy. I love Denni and I hope you let me see him still even after what I did to Bill Hamm because I had to take care of my brother!

## ...MISS ATHENA

Love is a lot like art... often imperfect
and fueled by trauma, but beautiful nonetheless.

Sometimes lovers are drawn
together by chance. Some are tied by fate.
For Cassius and Athena, it's a much darker
force that seems to bind them.

# ...MISS ATHENA

## -NOW-

Athena woke up in a panic. The cries of the child—desperate and afraid—echoed in the real world, or perhaps just in her mind, even as the dream faded. It had been a hazy, slipshod narrative that made even less now that she was awake.

There had been the baby of course, or at least its cries, and the maze of wheat from her childhood in Blackhaven. Cassius had been with her this time, holding her hand, and helping her navigate through the rows of crops. A black goat trailed behind them, its swollen udders dragging across the dirt. It let out goatish screams as it chased them.

She hated that she still dreamed about that place and of him. How long had it been? Over a decade. That was for sure. She knew she'd never be free from nightmares of Blackhaven, but it couldn't be healthy to still have Cassius taking up real estate in her mind as well.

She grabbed the water bottle from her nightstand, quenching her dry mouth, and tried to shake away the last foggy bits of her nocturnal thoughts. The wailing, that of a baby, started up again. She closed her eyes and bit her lip. The sound pierced her frontal lobe like a knife, twisted her heart, and left her body cold with fear.

Athena left her bedroom, not bothering to get dressed, and walked into the living room that served as her studio. There among the sheets of clay, wire skeletons, and half-formed bodies, was a sculpture she'd never made. The figure was fully formed and rendered—terrifyingly realistic. Its eyes were scrunched up in its bulbous baby head, its mouth wide in the species of indignant rage that only a small child can muster.

The baby's mouth never moved, but still, it continued to cry. Athena picked up a mallet from her toolbox and circled the sculpture. She admired its dimensions, the position of its limbs, and the folds of baby fat around its thighs. Its sparse hair—single strands so fine that clay shouldn't be able to replicate them—stood up in comic defiance of gravity.

There was something familiar about the child's features. She hadn't been able to put her finger on it the first few times she'd awakened to it, but now it hit her. The eyes. The lips. They belonged to Cassius.

Or maybe they weren't his. Maybe she was just projecting his features onto the sculpture. Babies all looked the same. People only thought they looked like their parents because of some trick of the brain—an artifact of psychology to keep caveman daddies from walking out on some kid who might belong to any other dude in the tribe.

Another cry issued forth from the static mouth of the sculpture. Athena raised her mallet and brought it down on the clay head, driving a thick line through its face. She hit it again and again, pounding the work of art until it was a silent and shapeless hump of clay.

-THEN-

Athena danced around the maypole, keeping time to the flute and the drums being played. Her skirt swirled around her bare legs and spring air felt wonderful on her skin. She was blindfolded with a strip of ivory linen, but the touch of the warm sun evoked images of blue skies and emerald fields bordered by rows of mammoth sunflowers. She'd always been good at conjuring images into her mind, down to the finest detail. She liked to draw the things she imagined. Mostly she used pens and pencils, but she dreamed of working with paints or clay. Before her mother died and her father had found his way to the commune, they'd gone to art museums in the city and her mind still went to those galleries every night. Art for the sake of art was frivolous though, and she knew there would be less and less time for it as she grew older. She was to be a wife and a mother. That was her fate and her calling.

She spun and jumped, holding onto the crimson ribbon attached to the maypole, a smile on her face. It was a happy day. It was her twelfth birthday, and she was surrounded by those she loved. The sun shone bright, the grass was soft beneath her feet, and she was the May Queen.

Athena tried to imagine the faces of the boys who encircled her. The All-Mother would soon guide her to one of them and they would be joined for life. Cassius was her first choice. He was cute and kind. She at least hoped not to get stuck with Remus the pants wetter or nose-picker Nero. Guilt washed over her for such thoughts. The All-Mother would guide her to her soulmate. Who was she to argue with divine wisdom?

She danced and hopped letting herself be moved by the whims of the music. She tried to remember that she had no say over her life. Every moment was pre-determined and had been waiting to happen since the beginning of time. Trying to influence providence was the highest form of sacrilege.

Athena's head felt light as she twirled through the grass, drawn away from the maypole. In her mind, she could see the All-Mother, guiding her forward. Her black fur and midnight horns stood in dark contrast to the springtime landscape of her imagination. Unborn kids struggled within the All-Mother, their hooves and horns pressing against her ever-pregnant belly. Yellow milk trailed from her swollen udders.

Athena half-danced and half-stumbled after the goddess in her mind. Her feet slipped and she fell laughing into the arms of a young man. She couldn't see who it was, but his frame was thin and his touch soft. He let out a concerned exclamation and tried to steady her, but they both toppled to the grass.

The rest of the commune, all set back behind the young men who circled the maypole, let out raucous cheers. Athena's heart pounded as she lay in the grass with the boy she'd just knocked down—the boy who would be her husband. The mixture of nerves and adrenaline caused her to break into a wild laughter, even as tears soaked into her blindfold.

She wanted to tear the strip of linen away from her face and look upon her betrothed, but tradition dictated that was his job, so she waited. Slender fingertips grazed her cheek. His hands trembled as he untied the knot and pulled the blindfold away from her eyes.

The day was too bright, after so many minutes with her eyes closed. She squinted and blocked the sunlight with one hand. When she could focus, she saw the young man staring at her, a nervous smile on his lips. The wind blew through his blonde hair, making it boyishly messy and his eyes shined like the springtime sky.

"Cassius," she whispered. She wanted to tell him that she'd hoped it had been him, but anxiety gripped the words in her throat and pulled them back inside.

-NOW-

Cassius stood in the spare room of his new apartment, examining the soundproofing he'd set up on the walls and ceiling, looking for any weak points. He cringed, thinking about fixing the walls when the time came to move and tear down the egg-crate foam, but that was a problem for future Cassius. For now, he had a studio again, and that was the important thing.

The soundproofing was as much for him as his new neighbors. Probably more for him since he programmed all his drums and played everything directly into his rig, rather than through amps. There was a baby upstairs, and he or she cried all night and day. Cassius guessed it was teething or colicky, and while he felt bad for the child and the parents, he also didn't want the little carpet gremlin's screeches showing up on his recordings.

With the room ready, he could now start unpacking and set up his computer, his rig, and his instruments. The setup was a little anemic. He'd been forced to sell a few guitars and components to pay for his divorce lawyer, but he'd build things back up. He'd always found a way to land on his feet, and he would this time.

Before Cassius could properly unpack and set up, he needed music. There was no internet yet, and he hated listening to stuff on the tinny speakers of his phone, so he set up an old boombox in the corner of the room and scavenged through a box of CDs and cassettes. He hadn't listened to most of it in years—demos from local hardcore bands and short-run pressings of metal bands that came and went without leaving a mark.

He thumbed through a stack of jewel cases, smirking at the amateur artwork and xeroxed band photos. He missed working on stuff like that. Most of it sucked, but it had a level of honesty and integrity that writing songs for other people lacked.

A burned CD-R inside a thin case stood out among all the other discs. *...miss Athena.* The words were scrawled across its face with magic marker.

"Holy shit!" he said, staring at his own handwriting. He hadn't seen the disc in years. He figured it had been lost in one of his many moves, but here it was.

He placed the disc into the boombox and hit play. After a few seconds of static and feedback, a guitar chimed in, playing a mid-paced arpeggio. He found his right hand picking at the air, remembering the pattern as if he'd played it just yesterday.

*Miss Athena, I've been wasting time with some pretty girl I'll never fall in love with …*

He cringed at the sound of his voice. It was an instant reminder of why he'd quit performing music and shifted his focus to writing.

*But she's fun to fuck and she's kind of cool, even if she doesn't compare to you*

*And maybe that's my problem dear, comparing earthly girls to angels so fair*

*And maybe I just can't forget the way I can't forget the taste of your breath*

"What the fuck, dude?" He shook his head at the lines … the crassness juxtaposed against cliche … the attempts to make repetition seem clever. Ugh. At least he was a better lyricist now.

His mind drifted to the girl the song was about. It didn't take the song to invoke Athena in his mind though. She was always there, which he knew was a little bit crazy, but they had been raised in a crazy manner and had shared a crazy adolescence.

They hadn't spoken in forever. They'd both moved on with their lives and left the insanity of their shared childhood and teenage years behind. Still, not a day went by that he didn't think about her. Neither time, distance, nor marriage and divorce had changed that. Was that romantic, obsessive, or the result of childhood trauma? He couldn't say, but he felt how he felt.

The arpeggio stopped and heavy open chords took over, leading toward the chorus. The change brought his attention back to the song, and he sang the next line along with the CD.

*And my whole life changed on that cold March day, you couldn't see my breath 'cause you took it away.*

Cassius smirked at the line. That one was pretty good, especially for a teenager. He opened his lips to sing the next line, but the speakers went silent and the disc made a whirring noise in the boombox. He reached to stop it, and the loud cries of a baby issued from the speakers. It was identical to the sound he'd heard from upstairs over the past few days.

He jabbed at the buttons but the CD kept spinning and the baby kept screaming. He swore and smacked the boombox, but it didn't cease. Finally, he pulled the cord from the wall.

The CD slowed to a stop. The display lights went out. The baby kept crying from the speakers.

-THEN-

Cassius looked around for the third time. The fields were bare, as the harvest had come and gone, so no one was working them. No grownups strolled down the dirt paths of Blackhaven to take in the last mild day before winter fortified itself for the coming months and all the little kids were inside for their daily lessons on math, reading, and religion.

"You're so nervous," Athena laughed. "It's fine."

Cassius nodded and opened the door to the old barn for her. The structure was abandoned. Deep cracks marred the brittle beams and sunlight crept through holes in the roof. It was slated to be demolished in the spring. For now, it was their special place—somewhere they could sit and talk about forbidden things—art and ideas from the outside world.

Cassius reached into his knapsack and produced an iPod and a pair of earbuds. He smiled and scrolled through the songs. He couldn't believe how many were on there and he hadn't heard of a single one.

"How did you get this?"

"The man who delivers the propane. I traded him some mushrooms for it."

"Cassius! The mushrooms are sacred!" Athena's tone was less angry than her words might imply, and the way she smacked his arm was more playful than anything.

"It's a good thing, then. I spread the faith. May he have beautiful visions of the All-Mother."

They laughed and Athena drew closer to him to look at the screen on the strange device. His body was warm and she pressed against him, as much out of affection, as to fight against the cold. Cassius offered one of the earbuds to her and chose a song at random. Distorted guitars came in, accompanied by simple but heavy drums. They both flinched at the sound, then giggled at one another, but kept listening. The tempo slowed and a man sang about fire, love, and sin, all in a simple catchy melody. Neither of them had ever heard anything like it, and it sparked something deep within Cassius' heart. He knew, right then and there, that his life would never be the same.

Athena was intrigued by the music, but she wasn't enthralled by it the way her betrothed was. The look in his eyes—the smile on his face—she had never seen him look so happy or so moved. It melted her heart to see him like that and she hated that this thing that brought him such joy would have to be a secret, and an unsustainable one at that. Someone would eventually find it, and that would be the end.

The song ended and Cassius put on another. It was a slower piece, played on a piano with a soft, tapping rhythm behind it. A beautiful baritone sang over the melody. The words of this one were more wholesome. It was a love song, plain and simple. No mention of fire or sin like the last song. No undercurrent of anger. It was just beautiful.

Athena laid her head on Cassius' shoulder. They swayed to the music, neither of them keeping rhythm very well and neither of them caring.

-NOW-

Athena slashed with her brush, leaving angry streaks of oil paint on the canvas. She was painting the goat from her dreams—Shub-Niggurath, the All-Mother. She hated everything about the creature. It's twisted horns. It's midnight hair and night-sky eyes. It's swollen, pregnant belly.

The painting was coming out rough and ugly—a fitting tribute to the All-Mother. She thought back to her childhood and how much that beast had taken from her. How her father fell under the spell of its cult and brought her to that backwater commune. The number the place had done on her and Cassius.

What had become of the other children of Blackhaven? Were they still toiling in the fields and praying to the stars for the coming of some terrible messiah? Had they been groomed and abused in the same way she and Cassius had been? Were any of the kids she grew up with chosen to replace them? The thought sickened her, but it wasn't her problem. She'd escaped, and that's all that mattered.

It was hot in her apartment and Athena had been painting in an absolute fury. Streaks and droplets of black and umber covered her clothes and skin, as well as the floor around her easel. She wiped the sweat from her forehead with the back of her hand, smearing splattered oil paint across her brow.

She stepped away from the canvas. The black goat looked at her with those impossible eyes where tiny white dots glowed amid a field of gleaming obsidian. It was a good painting. Monstrous and terrifying, but also beautiful. It was perhaps the best piece of art she'd made in some time, and she hated it.

Her eyes darted around her living room studio. A stack of paintings sat in one corner—a series of landscapes showing wheatfields and old barns with strange symbols. Tiny sculptures of crones and farmers lined one shelf. Her eyes fell to an abstract piece on the wall, and all she could think about was what she'd painted over to make that piece—a portrait of a teenage boy with a charming smile and stupid punk rock hair.

She'd spent all her life trying to escape Blackhaven, but had she? It was still all around her.

A terrible cry startled her, as if in answer to her question. She brought her attention back to the painting of the All-Mother. The goat was screaming, its painted mouth shifting open and closed against the canvas, but it didn't make the sound of an animal. Rather, it sounded like the crying of a baby.

Athena picked up the canvas and smashed it against the floor, breaking the wood it was stretched over and splattering paint all over the floor. She picked up the broken painting and threw it into the metal trashbin she used for old rags, then lit it on fire and watched it burn.

-THEN-

Spring was coming again. Both Athena and Cassius would be thirteen soon, and they were to be married on Beltane. On that evening, when the stars were right, they were expected to conceive their first child. Mistress Calypso, the Grand Crone, had said it was the will of the All-Mother, and that their child would usher in a new age.

Tonight, they would have their first lessons in intimacy. Together they would watch others perform the sacred marriage union so that they might know better how to please one another, as well as the All-Mother.

Julius and Sabina were firmly in their thirties, old by the standards of the pre-teens who had come to study their lovemaking. They were not entirely unattractive, Athena thought. Julius had the hard muscles of a man who'd been intimate with daily toil for all his life and Sabina was curvy and full-bodied. She didn't possess the polished sexiness that she remembered models on TV or in magazines having, but there was a genuine beauty to her that was more powerful than any manufactured glamor.

Athena and Cassius stood, hand in hand. They watched the older couple kiss and touch. They watched them make love and heard them moan and smelled their sweat and sex. It was alluring, terrifying, and intriguing. There was a magic to it, and as much as each of the children wanted a taste of such magic, they knew they weren't ready for it. It was too much ... too powerful.

Athena studied Sabina's naked form—the stretch marks from her pregnancies. The tired circles around her eyes. She admired her for being a mother, a wife, and a lover, but she wondered how much the woman had given up to be just that. Had she ever lived in the outside world? Was she haunted by unrealized dreams? Did she ever yearn for some identity beyond her biological function?

This was beautiful, but it wasn't what she wanted. There was a world beyond the commune—giant cities full of countless sculptures, nurtured gardens, and filthy streets. Children her age were out there, painting murals on the sides of buildings, playing music with their friends, and eating terrible, tasty food. That's what she wanted—a life of her own where she could experience the world and express it in art.

She looked over at Cassius and wondered if he felt the same. He had fallen so deeply in love with his secret music. Did he dream of leaving Blackhaven and buying a guitar? Were his dreams filled with record stores, rock concerts, and street performers singing in subways?

He squeezed her hand as if he knew what she'd been thinking—as if he was saying yes.

"Pay attention, dears," Mistress Calypso leaned between them and whispered. "This is just the first lesson. Soon you will lie with a mentor, so you may practice for your special night."

Athena swallowed hard as she watched Julius pin Sabina's arms over her head and work himself toward climax. She didn't want to be with him. She had no desire to be with anyone, except maybe Cassius. Even then, she wanted it on her terms, not like this.

-NOW-

Cassius looked at the run-down house in front of him, then double-checked the address on his phone. He was at the right place, and the thought kind of depressed him. The paint was peeling off the side of the house, the windows were blocked by brittle, cracking roller shades, and the yard was nothing but dead thorny bushes and weeds. It was no place for a kid to grow up. Then again, his childhood had been quite scenic, and he still had nightmares about it, so maybe appearances could be deceiving.

He pressed the doorbell, but it made no sound. After a few seconds, he knocked. A voice called from within, telling him the door was unlocked.

Cassius stepped inside and found the interior in as much disarray as the outside. Wallpaper was practically falling off the walls and the ceiling was blistered and yellowed from water damage. The living room was furnished with an ancient, stained couch and a beat-up coffee table. It reminded Cassius of a lot of the places he'd crashed as a teenager.

Sitting in a threadbare recliner was a thin young man with blond hair and piercing green eyes. He was holding a knockoff Stratocaster, softly strumming poorly formed chords.

"Hey, you must be Adrian."

The boy nodded and motioned for Cassius to take a seat on the couch. Cassius eyed the stains on the upholstery, but he sat anyway, not wanting to be rude. This was one of the reasons he'd quit giving guitar lessons in the first place. You never knew what you were walking into when you went to a stranger's house. He needed the money right now, however. The divorce had left him broke, and he needed to get back on his feet.

"So, what kind of stuff are you looking to play? Did you want to learn some songs, or focus more on theory and technique?"

"Maybe some songs?" Adrian asked.

"Sure, man." Cassius took his guitar out of its case. He plucked the strings, checking the tuning. "You have anything in mind?"

"I was thinking some Johnny Thunders, maybe."

Cassius eyed Adrian. He was young and didn't look particularly punk rock. Cassius was surprised the kid even knew who Johnny Thunders was. Then again, Cassius was too young for most of the music he listened to as well. Thunders had been in the ground for a decade before Cassius had heard his first distorted guitar. Age didn't mean a damn thing.

"Hell yeah, man." Cassius played the intro to his favorite Johnny Thunders tune. "What song?"

"That one, actually," Adrian said, recognizing the intro Cassius had just played.

"Good choice. Let's start at the intro, D to D suspended 4th. Like this."

Cassius showed Adrian the chords. The young man struggled with them, and his strumming was slow, almost like he was playing each note on its own. Cassius encouraged him, telling him he was doing good, but pointing out what he needed to fix. Adrian grinned at each bit of positive reinforcement. His smile was warm. The way he beamed, the shape of his teeth, and how his cheeks moved—it reminded him of Athena. She was the only person he'd ever know who smiled like that.

Cassius finished teaching Adrian the rest of the intro and listened to the kid play through it a few times. He was quickly getting the hang of it.

"All right. I'll play through the rest of it. You just watch my hands, and then we'll break it down piece by piece. Cool?"

"Cool."

The song was simple. Cassius had no problem remembering the chords or the lyrics. He closed his eyes and sang as he strummed. It was a sad song, but it always left him feeling a little bittersweet. It reminded him of how cold and alone he'd felt for a good chunk of his life—loneliness that no amount of sex, or alcohol, or even forced relationships could fill.

"And when I'm home, big deal, I'm still alone." He sang that line a little louder than the rest, probably because he felt it a little harder.

Images of Athena played out in his mind as he strummed the guitar and sang. He remembered her falling into his arms as she spun around the maypole and dancing with her to forbidden music in the old barn. He thought of sharing his first hotdog with her, her head on his shoulder on long bus rides, and the first time they'd kissed. He could almost feel her touch, but not quite. The song was right. You can't put your arms around a memory.

Cassius opened his eyes. And stared at his fretboard. He shook his head, knowing he needed to focus on teaching this kid guitar instead of getting caught up in his memories.

"So that's the whole song. You ready to break it down."

Adrian didn't answer. Cassius looked up and the boy was gone, along with his guitar. He called out his name and his voice echoed through the empty house.

-THEN-

Cassius' legs felt like rubber as he stepped off the bus. There were more people here than he'd ever seen, all so different. Grown men with arms like twigs and paunch beneath their shirts. Girls dressed in all black, covered in tattoos. People with skin tones like fertile soil. Others with hair the color of cherry blossoms.

Music played from overhead speakers in the bus terminal. Televisions mounted high on the wall played captioned sitcoms and news broadcasts. Dozens of new smells assaulted him, some evoking his hunger, others urging him to vomit.

A dark-skinned man in a wheelchair approached them. He talked too fast and loud for Cassius to understand what he was saying, but it was clear he wanted something from them. Athena rested her hand on

Cassius' shoulder and guided him away. His body trembled beneath her touch, and he took in deep, heavy breaths.

"It's going to be okay. I promise," Athena said, Squeezing Cassius' hand. "I'm here with you. I'm not going anywhere."

Cassius looked around, at all the people and the sea of lights. It was beautiful and terrifying. So much potential. So much danger. They would face it together.

"Ditto, kiddo."

-NOW-

Athena sat crying on the floor of her studio, her naked skin streaked with paint. She rocked back and forth as her works of art came to life all around her. Black goats called to her from painted landscapes. Statues of babies she couldn't remember sculpting wriggled with a life of their own, while sculptures of toddlers called out to her as their mother.

Portraits of Cassius sang to her from old sketchbooks—songs by Johnny Thunders and punk rock ballads she'd never heard. His husky, off-key voice was just as she'd remembered it—as charming as it was bad. She had tried to forget his voice like she'd tried to forget his face, and it was as heartbreaking as it was maddening to hear it now.

Athena covered her ears and closed her eyes. She prayed aloud for all of it to stop. She called out to Christ and Allah and any deity that would listen—any god that might take mercy on her. Only the All-Mother answered—her reply, a mockery of a child's cry.

-THEN-

"New Orleans."

Cassius and Athena were huddled together beneath an old blanket. It was cold in the abandoned record store they were squatting in. The heat didn't work, but luckily there was still electricity for the space heater they'd stolen and the boombox that had been left behind in the shop.

"Oakland."

He'd thought they'd gotten through the winter once February had passed and a few warm days rolled in, but he'd forgotten how cold March could be. This was a problem for him every year, going back to his earliest memories. The nearest hint of spring was so exciting to him that he forgot about winter until it blew its last frigid breaths upon him.

"Philadelphia."

"Phili?" Cassius asked, interrupting their game. "How can you even think of another cold city right now?"

"I didn't say I wanted to go there now. Maybe in June or July. Honestly, I don't care where we go, as long as it's not back home."

Nearly a year had passed since they ran away. A year of museums and punk rock shows. A year of big cities and Greyhound busses. A year of begging for change and stealing food. A year of surviving on the streets and seeing the world, with only one another to depend on.

"We should have gone further south," Cassius said, holding his hands in front of the tiny space heater.

"I don't mind the cold so much," she said, resting her head on his shoulder. That's what she said, but the sentence went on further in her mind. What she meant was *as long as we're together.*

"Do you ever regret leaving?" She asked. "Is it ever too hard out here?"

Cassius looked at their squalid surroundings. The mouse droppings on the floor. The holes in the walls and the water stains on the ceiling. His stomach grumbled and his toes ached from the cold.

Thoughts of full plates and warm fires back home came to mind. There were certainly things to miss about Blackhaven. He looked at Athena and remembered the look on her face the first time they went to an art gallery—how full of life her eyes were. They had never been like that in Blackhaven, and they never would have been.

A new song kicked in on the boombox. There was a slow arpeggio followed by warbling vocals. It was as ugly as it was beautiful and something he would never have heard had he stayed in the commune.

"No, I don't regret a thing."

### -NOW-

It had been days since Cassius last slept. The cries of babies and goats issued out from every speaker in his apartment—his boombox, his computer, his phone. Even speakers with no power, like headphones hanging on a rack, wailed for his attention.

Adrian sat on his bed, playing sloppy chords and out-of-time arpeggios on their own—mockeries of songs about love and heartache. Cassius wanted to yell at him—to demand to know what he was doing in his home and to kick him out, but he couldn't bring himself to do it. Every time he tried the kid would hit a chord just right and his lips would curl into a smile that lit up the room.

It was absurd to sit here and let this strange teenager play guitar in his room for days on end, but Cassius felt powerless. The thought of hurting the child's feelings—the thought of banishing that smile—it was too much to bear.

Cassius sat across from his bed, eyes raw and red, head heavy with the fog of exhaustion. Tears ran down his face as he wondered why this was happening and if it would ever stop.

### -THEN-

Cassius sat on a ratty mattress in the room he and Athena had been staying in, reading the letter for the seventh time. His tears had stopped, but he still trembled at every word.

*Dear Cassius,*

*Last night was beautiful. You're beautiful, but I can't do this. I know that you think you love me, and I feel like I love you too, but we were raised to think that. We were fucking programmed for this by our batshit crazy parents. I know it seems real, but it's not.*

*We ran away from that place so we could make our own destinies. I want to see the world and make massive sculptures and be a living statue in Central Park. I want to fall in love, on my terms, and I want to have my heart broken and break hearts and know that none of it is fucking pre-ordained.*

*And you—you should be joining bands and touring and playing music all over the world. You don't need to be handcuffed to some girl you grew up with. You don't need me hanging on you, like a chain to the past.*

*We both need to move on with our lives, and we can't do that with each other. It doesn't matter where in the world we go, if we are holding each other's hands, we are still holding onto Blackhaven.*

*I'm sorry to do things this way. I'm sorry to leave you alone. I think this is what we need, though.*

*I hope you have a beautiful life and that you forget all about me and the place we came from.*

*-Athena*

It was too unbelievable—too surreal. They had spent every day together for almost two years, traveling from city to city, fleeing their past. They'd run from cops and ripped off drug dealers. They'd laughed and cried and laughed some more, all the while falling in love, despite their best efforts not to.

And now, after all that time of fighting it, she was gone the morning after they gave in to their love. He could still smell her hair and her sex. He could almost taste her breath.

-NOW-

Athena drove down the old dirt road Blackhaven. Wheatfields blocked her view on either side, and she hadn't seen any sign of civilization in many miles. She had forgotten how secluded and remote the commune was. It made sense of course. It's hard to cut people off from the world if the world is in their field of vision.

The road twisted, then straightened revealing a series of rundown houses and barns, and a collapsed grain silo. Her hands trembled and nausea gripped her as she looked upon her childhood home. She didn't want to be there, but if she wasn't simply going mad and there were answers to what was happening to her, they would be here.

Even when she cut the engine and pulled the key from the ignition, the radio still played a cacophonous mix of Cassius' singing and wailing children for a few seconds more. She stepped out of the car and scanned the area. The fields were green and gold with life, but overgrown and untended. There were no signs of men working outside or women tending to their homes. Every structure was ill-maintained and in disarray.

Athena wandered through the commune, past the home she had grown up in and the fields her father had worked. She stopped at a clearing just past all the houses. A maypole stood there, a faded and ragged ribbon hanging from it. She took hold of it, and it occurred to her it was the first of May. How many years ago had it been since she'd danced in this very spot and fell into Cassius' arms? Twelve? Thirteen?

Holding the ribbon, Athena closed her eyes and danced around the maypole. She hadn't intended to, but something took hold of her. It felt good. It felt right. The insanity of the last few months evaporated like morning dew, leaving only joy and peace and the soft touch of sunshine on her skin.

She spun and twirled and laughed like a loon. Dizziness overtook her, but she refused to stop. She hopped and skipped and spun until she lost her balance and went tumbling away from the maypole. She braced herself for impact with the ground, but someone caught her.

Startled, Athena screamed and opened her eyes. What she was seeing was impossible. There was no way he was here.

"Cassius? Is that you?"

The question was rhetorical. There was no doubt it was Cassius who had caught her, not as the boy she remembered, but as a man, handsome and strong.

"What the hell are you doing here?"

"I was going to ask you the same thing."

Cassius helped Athena steady herself. They stood silent for the better part of a minute, staring at one another in disbelief. Over a decade of distance, yearning, and loneliness eroded as their gazes met.

"I umm … I was going through some stuff." Cassius broke the silence. "I think I needed some closure. About this place. About us."

"I'm sorry," Athena said. "You know, for how I left things."

"Don't be. We were kids, and maybe you were right."

Athena reached out and rested her fingertips against the back of Cassius' hand. She smiled. There was a sadness to it, but it still lit up Cassius' world like a supernova. He'd been dreaming of that smile for so long.

"I don't think I was right."

Cassius took Athena's hand, and they walked through the ruins of Blackhaven. Houses sat abandoned and the bones of animals lay in barns. There was not a soul to be found.

"What do you think happened here?" Cassius asked.

"I don't give a damn. The only thing I ever cared about in this place was you."

"Ditto, kiddo."

They wandered the grounds of the commune for hours, sometimes talking, sometimes silent, but never uncomfortable. As the sun fell behind the fields of wheat, they went back to the maypole and sat in the tall grass.

"So, what now?" Athena asked, squeezing Cassius' hand.

"Well, Blackhaven's a ghost town. Who knows what happened to our parents? There's no more cult to the All-Mother. Maybe we can try things again, on our terms, out from the shadow of Shub-Niggurath?"

"Maybe." Athena smiled, then pressed her lips against Cassius'.

No babies cried from the speakers of their cars. No black goats watched from the fields.

# DEADFALLS

The trees these boards were cut from have been dead a long time, so I don't have to worry about them... getting up and running off like in this tale.

Four camp counselors and their young troop have come to the woods to practice their survival techniques. They're about to discover that surviving will be harder than it seems when a boy goes missing, and only one man ends up left to tell the story of what lies undead in the forest...

# DEADFALLS

(RECORDING BEGINS)
[Several seconds of cacophonous ambient sounds]

had just closed my eyes when the kid came in screaming. It was Jason—Ken Barker's boy—the punk bastard who me and the three other adult chaperones/counselors had already reprimanded for pissing all over of the camp's communal bathroom building. He'd acted like a tough guy, even when we'd made him scrub the floor—the *entire* floor, shitty stalls too. Now he looked bloodless and batshit scared as he was shrieking about a tree that had swallowed Jeremy Bogdon.

Ed Claves and Tim Dropp had been playing cards by the light of a battery-powered lantern. The kid was hurt bad—they recognized the situation immediately, and moved to intercept him before the others could see. Ed was on one knee trying to calm him, while Tim stood like a bodyguard in front of them both, pushing back the other kids who were coming out of their bunks. I didn't know why Tim's face looked so pale at first, not until I saw Jason. His shirt was torn from the left sleeve down the front and the side of his face looked sort of chewed up, like it had skidded across gravel. His shoulder where his shirt was ripped was gashed pretty good, and I thought I could see meat. Jason didn't appear to have noticed it yet. If he had, he'd probably have passed out. I know I almost did.

Ed asked him, calmly, where Jeremy was. "It fucking *swalloooowed him!*" Jason shrieked. There was blood on his lips, in corners of his mouth running down his cheeks. I looked across the room at Rob Rovin, who was sitting up on his bunk, his crew cut unmoved by the pillow. He had been looking at Jason and now he looked at me.

"I've got you, buddy, okay?" Ed was saying over and over. Ed—was—a guidance counselor at Ridgelock-Central High School, and also a trained paramedic. Ed's own son Chris was one of the kids in the group. Of the four adults Ed was, needless to say, the best person to handle this, though this kid was way past a patching up with the cabin's first aid kit. He needed the hospital and fast.

"Listen to me. I need to know where you and Jeremy went," Ed said steadily.

"W-w-we snuck out," Jason said, sniffling. "Jerm-eremy had cig-aw-wu-rettes. We went to the woods an—"

His eyes rolled upward, then his head sort of dropped to one side and he saw his shoulder and started wailing like a toddler. Then the convulsions started. Tim looked over his shoulder at the kid and frowned. Behind me, I heard Rovin slide off the top bunk and land next to his boots. Tall boots, high laces, hooded gray jacket—a former soldier, called to duty. He pulled on a thin coat, then turned back and grabbed something from under his pillow and slid the object quickly into the inner pocket. He glanced at me, ticking his head towards the door. I grabbed a pair of flashlights and fell in step at once behind him. Tim gave us a quick nod, then started rounding the kids up, moving them away from Jason, who had stopped shaking and fallen into a sort of dazed half-sleep, giving Ed a chance to fully examine the kid's wounds. I glanced back at the others' faces as we walked out the door. I felt bad for them—they looked really scared, and we weren't telling them everything was okay like they expected us to. Like the adults are supposed to do, you know? Jesus Christ, if they'd actually had any idea what Jason had seen. What *I've* seen …

The night was full moon-lit, and the temp had dropped to probably the low 50s—cool for mid-August. I handed Rovin one of the flashlights and we flipped them on and started across the campground grass, grimly following Jason's blood trail towards the woods. I asked Rob:

"What do you think it was? That tore the kid up?"

Rovin said: "A bear I'm guessing. I hope the other one didn't suffer." At first, I thought he was talking about Jason, then I realized he was referring to Jeremy. He reached inside his jacket and clicked the safety off.

It started to rain, and I pulled my sweatshirt hood up and Rovin did the same. The path began at the parking lot east of the cabin, then ran parallel for a quarter mile along the border of the trees. We met it where it entered the woods and followed the blood trail left. The forest seemed denser than it had a few hours earlier when we walked it with the boys. There was a lot of noise going on in there now too—groaning and cracking that I wanted to attribute to the rain and wind but just couldn't.

About fifty yards or so ahead something was lying across the path. It looked like a downed tree, but the bark seemed to be creeping like the bristling back of an animal. Rovin watched it for a moment and drew his gun. I asked him what he was doing. He pressed a finger to his lips, then ran the beam along the trunk, stopping at the base. The exposed buttress roots were curled like a spider's legs around an object. Other thinner roots were slithering and piercing and retracing and plunging into the thing it was holding. Then the roots shifted and a leg slid free.

"What the *fu*—" I was starting to say when the gun went off—once, then twice, throwing splinters of (fleshy?) bark, up into the night. There was a howl, and the roots suddenly fanned out, releasing what they'd been holding, and the trunk—this is going to sound crazy—but it sort of S curved, then rose up, lifted by its buttress roots, and sort of scuttle/slithered horizontally backwards into the woods.

I remember saying something like "Man—that was no bear." We slowly approached the thing lying still in the path. Then we stood for a long time looking down at it. Jeremy Bogden was drown-white and there was a big hole in the center of his chest, ringed by a series of smaller ones poked into the soft places between his ribs, his throat, his groin. His eyeballs were pushed in. His jaw was cracked and cocked sideways. There was a bunch of teeth in the mud. I heard another half groan/half growl and pointed the flashlight into the trees. I didn't see anything but brown bark and pine branches. But seeing those made me think about what seemed to be missing. I remembered on our walk earlier in the afternoon that I'd seen a lot of dead-looking black trees standing amongst the others. I recalled thinking it was strange, and had even said something to Ed and Rob.

I turned to him then to mention it and at the same moment saw a dark curving line race out from the other side of the woods. It looped twice up Rovin's leg and pulled. I heard his shin snap as it wrenched him up and off the path, dragging him back into the verge on the other side of the road. When I saw him again he was lying at the underside of an upturned deadfall, which seemed to be quivering or twitching. I shined the light on it and saw that the center was gaping and there were what appeared to be rows of teeth—like fish bones sort of, but I guess they were wood, an unending vortex of them that seemed to stretch back and back into its "trunk"—and above the mouth two rolling eyes, lobster-like but of white like fungus. The roots around it were flailing around like tentacles. The "face" or whatever it was howled at me, even as it backed off slightly from my light. Jesus, that fucking sound. Then Rovin started wailing, and the thing turned back to him. Like a cat with a paralyzed mouse, it dragged him effortlessly back into the brush. As it did, Rovin feebly raised the gun and got a shot off, but it went wide. The thing hesitated a moment, seemed to consider him, then bent and sort of *planted* itself in his chest. Rob let out one long strangled warbling bray. It seemed to take him a long time to die—it seemed like a long time, but I think it was probably less than ten seconds. When he finally went still the thing grabbed him like a hand clenching a doll and pulled him back into the dark. Suddenly, behind me, I heard another howl—this time at my back.

I ran. It sounded like the whole forest coming down behind me, and I knew I was probably going to be dead within five seconds, but I ran anyway, and somehow made it to the camp's lawn. I could even see the cabin. It was darker on the western side of the little building. The edge of the woods was a lot ... *closer* than it had been only a few minutes earlier. It was pouring now, and the grass was slippery, and my clothes were sopping and sagged like weights, but I kept running and couldn't believe it when I reached the porch. Everyone looked up as I came in. The first thing I saw was Tim's face, which was graveyard solemn. Ed was sitting beside Jason Barker, who lay very still on the bed.

I said: "Ed, can I talk to you outside?" My voice was weirdly high and sounded kind of insane. Ed looked up, read something in my expression. He told the boys to stay put, told Tim he'd be right back. Tim sat on the bed, looking as spooked as the boys. Ed and I stepped out onto the porch.

"Where's Rovin?" he asked.

I peeked around the west-facing side of the cabin. The trees—if that's what they were—were only about fifty yards from the camp.

"We can't talk here," I said, and started towards the bathroom building before he could protest. He followed reluctantly, and when we were both inside I shut the door, bolted it, and then checked the clerestory windows to make sure they were locked too.

"What happened to Rob? Did you find the kid?"

"They're dead. Both of them," I said as I pulled off my drenched hooded sweatshirt and tossed it on the tiles.

Ed looked at me a long time, then he said: "Jason too. What is it, Darius?"

I told him what I'd seen.

"This isn't a joke, man. That kid in there is *dead!*"

"You think I'm playin'? So are Rob and Jeremy! And we got to get the fuck out of here, right now. Listen, I'm gonna get the van and drive it right up to the door. Get everybody ready and we'll load them up all at once."

Ed was saying something about it all being bullshit when we heard a sound like hundreds of people running outside. He frowned and opened the door before I could stop him. Long shadows were slithering/scuttling beyond. Then there was a sound like a tornado ripping the roof off the cabin. Then screaming.

"Ed, shut the fucking door!" I shouted.

He looked back at me and said, breathlessly: "Chris!" Then he was on his ass and being drug out onto the grass. He was gone before I could even think to reach out—it was that fucking quick.

I slammed the door, shut myself in this stall, and have been sitting here since. For a long time I pressed my hands to my ears, but the screaming got through ...

But it's been real quiet for a while now. I figure they're almost done with the kids, and with Ed and Tim. They'll smell me. I think their roots can taste us, sense us in the soil. They'll be coming here next. I've decided I'm going to try to make it to the van while they're still distracted. I think if I sneak around the south end of this building I might—

[Sound of shattering glass; shrieking; footsteps running off. Then: trotting footsteps, giving chase]
[76:04 seconds of silence]
(END OF RECORDING)

# AMBER HEAVENS IN LEADED GLASS

There are dreams older than you or I... phantom locales conjured by long-forgotten shamans and poets. Those ancient places still exist... even though they never existed. Each of us, even the biggest homebodies and hermits, can traverse fantastic ruins and alien worlds in our hours of sleep. The dreamlands are open to all.

But what if we brought something back with us? Something that didn't belong? Is there a price to be paid for stealing from our dreams?

# AMBER HEAVENS IN
# LEADED GLASS

Vinke, Brock - Session 1
October 2, 1951

Today I met with Brock Vinke for the first time. I had seen his
picture in the newspapers after the murder he'd been charged with
several months before. It was a vicious assault, and I am quite
surprised he was put into our care here at Danvers, rather than shipped
off to Charlestown State Prison. Maybe if the girl he'd killed, one Kerry
McNaught, had been better connected he wouldn't have gotten off with
an insanity plea. That wasn't the case, however. She was from the same
white trash stock as Vinke—an illegal immigrant living in the Irish
slums of South Boston.

It was clear from the newspaper clippings I had seen that Brock was
a large man, standing well above his public defender and the mobs of
reporters swarming him outside of the court. I was not prepared for the
reality of his size. His shoulders took up nearly the entire door frame
and he had to lower his head to pass through the entryway to my office.
His hands were like catcher's mitts, and I couldn't help but imagine

the terrible blows they were capable of delivering—the brutality those hands had unleashed to bring him here.

The orderly ushered Brock into a chair across from me, then left my office. I smiled but did not extend my hand. Patients here are too dangerous for handshakes. There is no telling how the deranged mind might react to even such a simple gesture. Instead, I introduced myself and asked how he would like to be addressed.

I was met with silence. I stared into his eyes, trying to read if he was willfully ignoring me, if he was lost in his own mind, or if there was anything at all going on inside his skull. Those glassy, gray eyes—the color of a stormy horizon—conveyed no information to me. He simply stared, as if looking beyond me.

I decided to call him by his given name, rather than his surname since he gave me no answer on how to address him. This was not out of disrespect, but rather an educated guess on what a man such as he might prefer. A firmly blue-collar longshoreman, I imagined that addressing him less formally would make him more comfortable.

I looked through Brock's paperwork on my desk, including transcripts from his trial. He never spoke a word in his own defense and his lawyer had argued that he was catatonic. The only words he spoke at all during his trial came in the form of accusatorial outbursts toward jurors and lawyers. The outbursts were stricken from the court record, but the public defender's notes revealed them to be grotesque and outlandish condemnations.

I next asked Brock if he knew why he was here and how he had come into my care. I was reluctant to bring up his victim just yet. I didn't know if her name might induce his rage, and it is better to ease into these things, in my experience. This question, like the last one, got no reply. Brock's unresponsive eyes just gazed forward.

For the sake of clarity and professionalism, I read the jury's verdict and the judge's sentence aloud. It is important that patients understand what brought them here. Oftentimes it is necessary to repeat this exercise over and again before criminal patients begin taking responsibility for their actions. I fear that Brock Vinke may be too far gone for that, however.

I could be wrong. I've seen seemingly worse-off patients turn around with care and determination. I don't anticipate that Brock Vinke will ever be rehabilitated, but perhaps he can find some semblance of meaningful existence here at Danvers State.

### Vinke, Brock - Session 2
### October 9, 1951

Today was my second session with Brock Vinke. Nurse Gibbons tells me that he has been unresponsive in his group sessions and in general. She finds his mannerisms, or lack thereof, as unnerving as his size. It is scary to have a patient of such size and strength. The orderlies are anxious around him as well, I've been told, though he has exhibited no aggressive tendencies.

Once a week isn't enough time to spend with a non-responsive patient with a history of violent outbursts. I should be working to trigger his rage so that we might pinpoint its cause. We'll get there eventually. My goal today was to make him feel more comfortable. He'll never open up if he's too nervous.

I began our session by re-introducing myself and asking if he remembered me. As was the case last week, he did not respond. Expecting this, I followed up with a few other simple questions.

Could he state his name?

Did he know the year and the month?

Could he tell me who won the last world series?

Silent, his eyes stared through or perhaps beyond me. It was as if I didn't exist. I followed his gaze to the wall behind my desk. He seemed transfixed on the art print framed on the far wall.

"Is this what you're looking at, Brock?" I asked, pointing toward the picture. It was a painting of a doorway, scarred and battered, its dimensions neither level nor plum. A wreath of flowers hung upon the door, and while the pink of the petals was vibrant, it somehow melted into the muted contrast of the other subject matter.

"Do you like it? The artist's name is Ivan Albright, and the painting is called *That Which I Should Have Done I Did Not Do*, but most just call it *The Door.*"

"It's almost right," Brock muttered.

I marked down his words immediately. They were few, but I thought it important to make sure I had them exact, and not allow memory to distort this first interaction. Given his barrel chest and the dimensions of his body, I'd expected a deep, booming voice. This was not the case. He spoke softly, his words slow and deliberate.

"What's that?"

"It's almost right," he repeated. "The door."

"What do you mean?"

"It's narrow like that, but taller. The closer you get, the taller it gets.

"You've seen this door before?" I looked for some change in expression, but his face stayed impassionate.

"Yep. The color ain't quite right neither. Ain't that fella's fault. I ain't never seen the color of that wood nowhere else."

"Where have you seen this door, Brock?"

"We all seen it. It's the door to dreams. Some 'member it. Some don't. I 'member it better than most, I reckon."

I was intrigued. I'd seen patients fixate on pieces of art before and I'd seen them make up stories around such works, but never a mind so primitive as Brock Vinke. I wondered for a moment if I had misjudged him. Perhaps he was more than an oafish dock worker.

"Are you an art lover, Brock? Do you go to museums? Or perhaps draw?"

"Don't care much for paint or pencils, but I like beautiful things. Looking out to sea when there's no telling the ocean from the sky. The rainbow colors on a wet clam shell. The way that mist clinging 'round crumbly old cities captures the moonlight like a net."

I paused at this last statement. Crumbly old cities? What ruins could this dock worker from South Boston have seen? I wondered if perhaps he'd taken a day trip to Dogtown or some other New England ghost town.

"Crumbly old cities? What do you mean by that, Brock?"

"Old places where the buildings are all stone. Not brick, all laid out neat, but made up of rocks of all different sizes. Most of those places ain't much more than rubble now. Maybe they was always rubble. You can tell what some of 'em were supposed to be. Ocean-gray steeples sticking out from piles of stone. Statues with faces worn smooth like sea glass standing guard outside rusted gates.

"And like I said, there's the mist. The way it glows black and silver like it stole just a bit of the light from the moons and the dark stars in the yellow sky. It's like it's breathing. The silver light gets real bright, like the cherry at the end of a cigarette, then it fades as the black gets … well not quite brighter, but …"

"More intense.' I whispered, not meaning to speak.

"Yep. You know what I mean."

I did know what he meant. I had seen it before, everything he described. The ruined temples and the faceless idols. The pulsing fog. The twin moons against a yellow sky, speckled with dark stars that radiate unlight.

My arms erupted with goosebumps and my pen slipped from my trembling fingers. I placed my hand down on my pad and found the paper turned moist at my touch.

My mind reeled, grasping for some logical explanation as to how my patient could describe this fantastic place I'd dreamt of so many times. Was it inspired by some real place we'd both seen on postcards, or in a newsreel? Was it something archetypal, in the Jungian sense—a shared dream across mankind? Was my psyche allowing him to fill in the blanks of my half-forgotten nocturnal journeys?

"Where is this city, Brock? How did you come across it?"

"Same place you seen it." Brock nodded toward the Albright painting. "On the other side of the door."

## Vinke, Brock - Session 3
## October 16th, 1951

I have gone through all of Brock Vinke's files again and have done my best to conduct as full a history as I can on him. He is a second-generation American, descended from Dutch and Irish immigrants. He inherited neither money nor respect from either side of his family.

According to Brock, he has never left Massachusetts and has worked as a longshoreman since he dropped out of school at fourteen years old. I have no reason to doubt him, and his former employer confirmed that Brock had never taken a vacation in all the years he worked for him.

Additionally, the patient is devoid of culture and barely literate. While he can read enough to get by in life as a laborer, he can't make his way through so much as an article in The Globe. There is no way he could have explored the works of fantasists like Howard or Dunsany that might have inspired his imaginings of ruined cities and impossible skies with twin moons.

Might he have spent his leisure hours in museums, around antiquities and images of bygone days? Could some Saturday matinee epic have put such ideas in his head? Or, as I hypothesized before, has Brock tapped into some stream of the collective unconscious?

The answers to these questions will have to wait. There was an incident that we had to talk about this week instead. Brock had a violent outburst, similar to the one that caused his incarceration. This time his victim was another patient, and luckily made of sturdier stuff than the woman he murdered. Still, the poor man will be in the infirmary for at least a week.

Sometimes the sedate way Brock carries himself makes me forget just how dangerous he is. I wonder if this is purposeful—a method for disarming his victims. It seems a sophisticated ploy for a man of his limited intellect, but the nefarious often comes naturally to the simple and the poor.

When he was brought to me, Brock had several visible bruises and lacerations. The guards, no doubt, were rough with him due to his intimidating stature. Despite this, his expression revealed neither anger nor shame, just that dreamy, somnambulant gaze.

"I understand there was an altercation between you and Mr. Schraft," I said, trying to hide any judgment in my voice.

"He's a bad person," Brock replied, his voice calm. As with our last two sessions, his eyes were focused on the Albright painting.

"Why do you think Mr. Schraft is a bad person?"

"I seen the bad things he done. Touched on kids. Hurt 'em. Broke 'em."

Brock was right. Schraft was a pedophile, tried and convicted. Only the wealth and connections of his parents allowed him to be sent here rather than serving a harsh sentence at Charlestown Prison.

"What makes you think that? Did you hear someone make such an accusation? Did Mr. Schraft tell you this?"

"Know it the same way I know most things. Dreams."

I jotted down a few notes—questions about Brock's sincerity. Did he truly believe that his dreams offered special insight into the secrets of others? Perhaps he had gotten wind of Schraft's dark proclivities and subconsciously attributed that knowledge to his dreams. Or perhaps he was intentionally constructing a narrative, like some crude storyteller. He certainly seemed to have the imagination of a fantasist, despite his otherwise base mind.

"Are you telling me you beat a man bloody over a dream, Brock?"

"That painting," Brock motioned toward the Albright print. "Some fella took that image from a dream and captured it.

"It works both ways though. Folks can scribble their hopes and sins onto dream, like kids drawing with sidewalk chalk. They barely know what they're doing. Their hands start moving and their secrets come out."

"Even if that's true, how is it you're privy to Mr. Schraft's dreams?"

"Because the door never closes for me. I've always got one foot in and one foot out. I see things others don't."

"Is that why you killed that girl? Were her sins revealed to you in a dream as well?"

Brock looked down at the floor. His eyes welled up with tears. It was the first time I'd seen any emotion cross the man's face. My body tensed, as I was unsure if these were tears of sorrow or rage. I suddenly became acutely aware of how little effort it might take for Brock to kill me if he so chose. Even with the orderly standing guard outside my office, I suspect he could easily break my neck before being subdued.

A moment passed and I watched his lip tremble, ever so slightly. He was sad, rather than angry. Relief washed over me.

"That was an act of mercy. Needed to set things right. Kerrigan didn't belong here. The world was changing her ... killing her."

"The world didn't kill that girl, Brock. You did."

"I never should have brought her through the door. Dreams are never right on this side of things. That's why I don't like pictures or music. It's always wrong ...just a little bit off, at best ...

"Told you I love beauty, and I ain't never seen nothing as beautiful as Kerrigan. Her eyes shifted colors, like her soul burned blue and green. The black stars painted sooty streaks against her fiery hair. Nothing in this world could compare—not the skyline at night, or the ocean at dawn.

"Selfish and stupid, I brought her back with me. She wasn't made for this world, and I shoulda known it. Being here did things to her. I could see the poisons of this place taking her over ... hate and jealousy ... booze and smoke ... time and sickness ..."

Brock wiped a single tear from his cheek. Many of my patients cry in performative ways. They use it as a manipulation tactic. I don't believe this was the case with Brock.

"Kerrigan? Do you mean Kerry McNaught? The woman you murdered?"

"It was wrong of me to take her from the dream. I ruined her, so it was up to me to fix her … to send her home, the only way I knew how."

**Vinke, Brock - Session 4**
**October 23rd. 1951**

Brock Vinke is insightful to an uncanny level. It's amazing how much he is able to pick up on from people, especially given his limited intellect. Aside from being able to glean information about the crimes of his fellow patients, Brock has spooked several members of the staff, confronting them about their sins and secret thoughts.

This has led to several more physical altercations, but with Brock on the receiving end of the violence. One of the orderlies took special offense when Brock accused him, in a detached and disinterested way, of desiring other men over his wife. This earned him a few more stitches than he had last week.

I decided to explore this ability more deeply today and invited Brock to share any insights he might have about me. Normally, I wouldn't recommend opening oneself up to a patient in this way, but it was the most efficient method for me to gauge the accuracy of his insights.

"Last week, you said that your dreams gave you special knowledge about people. I'd like to explore that a bit more. Do you have any insights about me?"

Brock didn't answer. He simply stared at the Albright print, same as always.

"Brock?"

"Folks don't care to hear what I know," he said, running his fingertip along his stitched-up eyebrow.

"Are you afraid you'll get in trouble? I promise you won't. This room is safe, Brock. You can say whatever you like here."

He shook his head. His eyes were dreamy and bloodshot. I had seen this kind of behavior before—patients retreating further into themselves as the hospital began to break them. Sometimes it's mistreatment from the staff. Other times it's a sense of the outside world passing them by.

Most often it's giving into the collective madness that permeates a place such as this. It creeps over staff and patients alike. We have tried to make Danvers comfortable and rehabilitative, but mental illness echoes through these halls. It ripples out sending disturbances through each of our minds. Some are equipped to handle it. Others are not.

"Humor me. Please, Brock. I promise I will not get angry."

Brock turned toward me. We locked gazes and a look of deep consideration crossed his face. I'm unsure of what he was thinking in that moment. Maybe he was trying to look for dark secrets hiding within me. Perhaps he was taking measure of my character and deciding if he could trust me not to lash out if his insights offended me.

"I've seen you, in the old city beyond the door. You ain't dragging sin in behind you the way Shraft did, but you wear your lonesome like a robe, and your veins probe the ground like thirsty roots, but they can't find no purchase.

"I seen you forage through the rubble, looking for answers to questions you ain't never thought of asking. It feels familiar to you— the crumbly old buildings painted silver and black by the moons and the stars. It's not your home, but it's maybe the closest you ever felt to having one."

I went to jot down what he'd said, but my hand was stricken still. Brock's words were chillingly accurate. I had dreamt of that place he spoke of—that crumbly old city, as he put it— since I was a child. It was such a constant fixture of my dream-life that it often felt more real to me than any place in the waking world. My mother moved us around so much as a child that we never put down roots. That listless feeling stuck with me through college, as I switched roommates from year to year. Even to this day, I find the idea of owning property or being tied up in a marriage to be stifling propositions.

Moreover, he was correct about me searching for answers to questions I hadn't asked. I have spent countless nights examining that dream place. In my sleep, I roam the broken streets of the doomed and forgotten city, for which I have no name. Tendrils of black unlight descend from the stars and the heavy mist pulses with the silver radiance of the twin moons.

It's as if I'm an archeologist, looking to piece together an impossible puzzle from slivers of leaded glass and worn sigils. Artifacts buried beneath the ruined temples and engraved histories, now lost time and erosion taunt me. The golden faces of forgotten kings stare at me from ancient coins. Secrets are whispered through the mist, in a tongue I can't comprehend.

Awake, I record those dreams and psychoanalyze them, looking for meaning and subtext in the imagery and the action. The mystery is just as intense in my conscious hours, as I pull back layers of metaphor and archetype.

"The problem is you never see quite right in your dreams." His voice was soft and matter-of-fact. "You never see the city for what it is because your vision's all blurred. It's like your eyes work just fine, but you put on spectacles to look smart, even though the moonlight glares on the lenses and they make you dizzy."

"I don't quite follow, Brock."

"Most folks don't. That's why they can't get to the places I go or see the things I see."

"But you know I've been to the ruins of the city behind the door." It's irresponsible to feed into a patient's delusion, but this must be more than that. There is so much truth in what he says. "You've seen me there, in that doomed and forgotten city."

"There are countless places far beyond those ruins." He spoke with the dispassion of a sleepwalker. "Shores where monsters play beyond reefs and sandbars. Fields where rabbits swim through tall grass as hills move like waves 'cross the horizon. Old docks where pirates hang in cages and whisper secrets and lies to any folks who'll listen."

"Well yes, there are countless dreams. They are as limitless as human imagination."

"Limitless … that's the right word. They are limitless, and I can see 'em all."

## Vinke, Brock - Session canceled
## October 30th. 1951

The hospital was wild tonight. There are always more incidents of violence and self-harm around Halloween. It makes me wonder about the history of the holiday, and what archetypal role it fulfills within the human mind. Why have we in the West cultivated these gruesome communal traditions and celebrations of the macabre?

We try our best to keep things normal during Halloween at Danvers State, while allowing the patients to have some sense of festivity. Nothing too scary. No disturbing monster movies or violent radio plays. We let them make decorations and paint Jack O' Lanterns (we can't allow them knives to carve them), and we supply costumes for those who might like to dress up.

Even this minimal level of celebration can be too much for some of our patients. It seems, unfortunately, that Brock Vinke was among that number. We were supposed to have a session today, but the man was catatonic.

As morning gave way to afternoon, Brock became less and less responsive to the staff. Offers to join in activities were met with blank stares. He would not participate in group therapy or rise to wait in line for his afternoon meds. Mr. Schraft, noting Brock's unresponsive state, took the opportunity to burn his hand with a cigarette in retaliation for the beating he'd received. The patient who witnessed and reported this incident claimed that Brock did not so much as flinch as the ember of tobacco seared his skin.

His condition did not improve throughout the day. Two large orderlies had to move his massive form into a wheelchair and lift him into bed for lights out. I truly hope this is a temporary and fluke occurrence. Despite Brock's mental shortcomings, he is extremely insightful and in possession of a rich imagination. I would hate to see that extinguished by some species of creeping catatonia.

I took advantage of the time I would have spent with Brock to review my notes from our past sessions, including his other files. Upon review of our conversations, I find myself dumbstruck by the insights he is able to glean about others—what he can tell about their hopes, transgressions, and their literal dreams. It is truly uncanny.

It seems impossible, but I believe Brock, as simple as he is, holds a deep and accessible connection to the collective unconscious. What an incredible gift to possess, if that's truly the case. Imagine the possibilities of cultivating such an ability.

I will be doing more testing to determine if Brock Vinke's gifts are preternatural, or if he is simply skilled at picking up on subtle cues that others miss. I don't quite know how to determine that yet, but I will spend the weekend designing a methodology and experiments. The thought of what stands to be proven leaves me trembling with excitement.

On a separate but related note, I have dreamt of that nameless ruined city every night since my last session with Brock. I can't shake the thought of what he said, how I am unable to see it accurately through the lenses I wear.

Could he be correct? Is there an objective reality to a shared dream—a clear view of the ethereal that only the gifted can behold?

I find myself daydreaming about his fantastical claims that the McNaught girl was some dream that he'd stolen off with and brought into the real world. Dare I try that with a shattered tablet or slivers of leaded glass? Might I get a more accurate view of this place if I could manage to sneak a piece of it back to the real world? I contemplate this each night that I manage to return to the nameless city, but the featureless gazes of the city's monolithic guardians warn me not to take anything away from those sacred grounds. Still I try, but the artifacts slip from my hands as I wake and I lose attunement with the dream.

**Vinke, Brock - Session 5**
**November 6, 1951**

I am happy to report that Brock broke out of his catatonia the day after Halloween. He was responsive again, though he remained quiet and distant, only speaking when spoken to, save for some cryptic comment here and there. This is normal for him.

I suspect that Brock's indifference to verbal communication stems, at least in part, from his years spent working on those wretched docks in the squalor of South Boston. Who would want to try and talk over the sound of engines and cranes, along with the squawk of gulls? And what manner of conversation was to be had among such company? The exchange of mindless vulgarities occurring at such a place must have held little interest to one with such a rich imagination. And Brock is so naturally sensitive to others, that I imagine he avoided such company, so as not to pick up on the crude dullness of those around him.

It must have been hard, having such an intense imaginative faculty, and no way to express it—no one to share such visions with. To have such an intimate understanding and familiarity with the world of dreams, and such a connection to the undercurrent of human consciousness, yet find oneself so alone in the waking world ... it turns a blessing into a burden.

Worse still, poor Brock lacks the critical intelligence to fully understand his unique gifts. It is poetically criminal that a man with no drive and of such otherwise low mental faculties should have such sensitivity bestowed upon him by God. He is simply not equipped to tend the ember of greatness within his soul. No wonder the poor bastard went mad and ended that poor girl's life.

As much as I lament Brock's inability to understand the nature of his unique aptitudes, I find myself nearly as perplexed by them as he must be. While I understand that his insights aren't mystical and that the dream worlds he speaks of are but symbols, it is unheard of for an individual to be so naturally tapped into the collective psyche. If I can understand where his sensitivity stems from, or even begin to glean its true nature, I will have opened the door to a whole new realm of psychology.

With that goal in mind, I have conducted an experiment during today's session. Instead of a typical therapeutic discussion, I had Brock meet me in one of the group counseling rooms, along with two patients from the women's ward and Mr. Hann, a patient who Brock has spent substantial time around.

My hypothesis was that Brock subconsciously picks up on subtle signals from people as he spends time around them, and his mind transfers the data he has absorbed into universal symbols. These symbols provide a sort of theater in his mind, where the hopes and sins of others play out before him.

I tested to see if Brock can tell me as much about people he is completely unfamiliar with, thus the patients from the other ward. As for Mr. Hann, who shares a floor with Brock, he was my control for the experiment.

There was a general sense of discomfort from all the patients involved when the experiment began. New situations can often agitate the mentally unstable. The female patients seemed particularly tense. Perhaps it was the presence of so many unfamiliar men—Brock, Mr. Hann, and myself. Perhaps it was Brock's size. Or maybe it was just the fragile nature of the nervous, feminine mind.

Mr. Hann was also quite unnerved. I chose him in part because I knew that he had an aversion to women and wrestled with self-loathing and latent homosexual tendencies. Placing him in a room with women would make him all the easier for Brock to read. I predicted that Brock would be able to accurately attest to Mr. Hann's aberrant sexuality and that he would draw a blank on those people whom he had not spent any time around.

Brock, out of everyone in the room, myself included, was the least tense. In possession of that sleepy calm that only left him in his fleeting moments of violence, he raised no questions about the change in venue, or about the others brought into his session. He did glance around more than usual, but with a sluggish curiosity rather than a sense of concern.

"Brock, we are going to play a little game today, if that's all right with you."

He nodded his head, slowly scanning the walls of the room, all but looking through myself and everyone else gathered around the table. He did not seem uncomfortable, but I sensed the slightest melancholy in his glassy eyes.

"Is everything all right, Brock?"

"I like your office better," he muttered.

"Why is that?"

"It reminds me of home."

For a moment I was offended. I take pride in my office. It isn't particularly luxurious, but I like to think that I maintain a level of sophistication in my workspace. What could the squalid room that Brock rented near the docks of South Boston have in common with my own sensibilities?

My indignation faded as the true meaning of Brock's words found footing in my mind. He was not speaking of my office itself, nor of whatever shabby place he had rested his head before coming to Danvers. What he missed was the Albright painting in my office, and the home he spoke of was the dream world beyond it.

"Brock, I'd like you to give us your insights on everyone in the room, starting with Mr. Hann, and moving along to the right. Can you do that for me?"

"People don't like what I have to say," Brock muttered, unbothered by the statement.

"This is a safe place, Brock. Your insights are welcome here. No one will get mad or violent."

Brock turned his lazy eyes toward Mr. Hann. He regarded his fellow patient for several seconds and offered a rare smile. It appeared to be not a smile of happiness, but an expression meant to comfort another. It seemed incredibly empathetic, but should I be surprised? Brock is quite sensitive.

"Go on," I urged

"I've seen you in the dream, Mr. Hann," Brock said. Mr. Hann swallowed hard, and his hands became restless. "You search for love each night. Sometimes you call out a name in the crumbly city just past the door. Other times you whisper at the sea, praying for the waves to bring back someone you lost ... or maybe you never had 'em in the first place."

"Can you be more specific, Brock? Is there anything ... unusual about Mr. Hann's dreams?"

Mr. Hann shifted in his chair, shaking with nervous energy. He knew what I was getting at and wished for it to be kept silent. I shouldn't have nudged Brock like that. It can influence the experiment to do so, but I needed to know if he could glean Mr. Hann's homosexual tendencies.

"Nothing strange. Same kinda dreams as a lot of other folks. Lots more than you might suspect."

Was Brock implying that Hann's perversions were more commonplace than one might think, or did he not see them? I jotted down a few notes in my pad and we moved on to the next patient, a woman named Penelope Waters. Waters was admitted by her husband after their only child died. She is completely non-verbal and only communicates via single words spelled out in scrabble tiles. She is, in my opinion, completely incurable, so we try to keep her mind numb and comfortable through medication.

"And what about Mrs. Waters? Can you tell me anything about her dream life? About her hopes?"

Brock regarded Mrs. Waters for a moment, then shook his head. I felt a spark of excitement come alive in me. Brock was unable to tell anything about this woman and for a moment I thought my hypothesis was holding water. Even as I wrote down this finding, Brock shattered my theory and amazed me all at once.

"I can't tell you nothing, 'cause nothing's there," Brock said. "She don't hope. She don't dream. She don't sin. Poor thing's barely there at all. The door to dreams won't even open for her."

Incredible! Without ever meeting this woman, Brock could feel that her connection to the greater consciousness he was so intimately tied to was severed by the drugs in her system. He could sense that she was isolated and adrift in a sea of sorrow and madness. His sensitivity was greater than I had anticipated.

Results were impressive with the third subject as well. Brock was able to tune in on the guilt which plagued the other female patient, a widow who blamed herself for her husband's suicide. He spoke of her crying beneath a swinging corpse in a forest of leafless trees. She broke into hysteria as he described the tree being fed by her tears, growing taller each night, taking her deceased husband further from her and higher into the black night.

I was tempted to have Brock continue with the orderly, but I feared for both of their safety. If some horrible or embarrassing secret were revealed aloud, violence might erupt. I am far too slight to stop either of those men if they were determined to do harm to one another. Best to keep the staff out of such experiments.

Vinke, Brock - Session 6
November 13, 1951

One of the many things that perplexes me about the case of Brock

Vinke is the speed at which he is able to analyze others and speak their dreams aloud. The fact that he can do this at all is amazing, but it seems so effortless. He need not hear them speak or even watch their body language for any considerable amount of time.

My initial hypothesis that he was subconsciously picking up on cues and bits of conversation, then transferring them into the universal language of symbols seems disproved, in light of last week's experiment. Brock is simply in touch with the world of dreams and symbols, in a seemingly impossible way. I'm reluctant to go so far as to call his gifts mystical, but I can't think of another term that quite fits. It sounds like hogwash, I know, but what other answer is there?

I have tried to reach such a connection with the realm of the nocturnal mind for many years, going back to my days at University. Colleagues have teased me for my interest in lucid dreaming. Some have looked down on my use of mushrooms and other illicit substances to reach altered states of consciousness. Nothing has brought me close to the level of attunement that my patient has found. To not only travel through worlds of my own making at will, but to step into the dreams of others ...

Over the past week, I have returned to exercises I practiced in my youth. Meditation techniques as well as the use of external stimuli have helped me reach deeper into the world of the immaterial. Under such circumstances, I have returned each night to the ruins of the city beyond the great door. Beneath the coiled glow of the moons and the unlight of the contrasting stars in the vast amber sky, I traversed the crumbling hillside temple, searching for tracks left by other dreamers—paths to secret grottos and haunted houses and beaches where lavender waves crash upon charcoal shores—places where I might spy their secrets. No roads were open to me.

"How do you do it, Brock?" That was the first question I asked this session.

Brock was slow to answer even though we were back in my office and there were less distractions. His half-closed eyes were focused on the Albright painting. He looked less present than normal—somehow dreamier than in our past sessions.

"How do I do what?" He asked.

"How are you able to touch the dreams of others? How can you look upon their secrets? Their fears and fantasies?"

"I don't try. I'm just drawn to 'em. Their dreams pull me in, like a riptide." His words were slow and soft. "Or maybe I'm the riptide, pulling 'em in."

"Why you? Is there a drug you used perhaps? Or a head injury? Did you learn dreaming techniques handed down through your family? Or from a learned immigrant from some exotic land you may have met on the docks?"

Brock's laugh was almost imperceptible. It was the first time I'd heard him find humor in anything. A flush of embarrassment crossed my face as I realized how absurd my questions were ... thoughts borrowed from pulp magazines and Saturday matinees.

"There's no secret. Least if there is, it ain't found in a book or a pill or a tonic."

"Then why can't I do it, Brock? Why can you alone touch dreams?"

"I'm sure I ain't the only one. You could do it. Anyone can."

"I've tried! I've tried for years, long before I met you."

"Maybe that's the problem. You try too hard. Dreams ain't made of ten-cent words. They can't be mapped out or turned into 'rithmetic. You can't buy their magic from a druggist." Brock rubbed his eyes, looking as if he might fall asleep in the chair. "Dreams are made of sand and seagull calls. Children's laughter and moonlit waves. They're made of sex and death and all the beautiful things in between."

I found myself getting agitated. Brock's romanticism often seemed charming to me, especially juxtaposed against his imposing stature and inconsiderable intellect, but I found myself annoyed by it in that moment. It wasn't his fault that he could not share his methods with me. They were no doubt a secret to him as well. Of course, he would default to storybook sentimentality. That was a common crutch of the poor and uneducated.

"And how do you connect with the dreams of those you just met, like the widow from our session last week?" I asked, deciding to shift the conversation a bit, "You were both awake? How do you touch someone's dream life when neither of you are sleeping?"

"Our bodies stay in our beds while we sleep, but the world still goes on 'round us … even though we ain't awares. Folks can see us in our beds. They can watch us. Touch us. Hurt us. Right, doc?"

I nodded, conceding his point, not sure where he was going with it.

"It's the same the other way 'round. Our dreams don't go away when we wake up … we just ain't awares."

"That's an interesting concept, Brock, but it doesn't answer my question. How can you access the dreams of others from the waking world?"

"I did answer. You ain't listening." There was no anger or judgment in his voice. It was a simple, impassionate statement. "We're always in both places. One foot in the dream … one foot on the earth. Most folks just can't see that."

## Vinke, Brock - Session Cancelled
## November 20, 1951

I canceled my session with Brock today. To say that I am currently overwhelmed would be a grand understatement and I fear that perhaps I'm going a bit mad. My preoccupation with dreams has become all-consuming since my sessions with Brock Vinke began. His gifts seem nonsensical—fantasies from the realm of bad fiction. But how can I deny what I have seen?

Brock's most insane claim is that he pulled the McNaught woman from a dream. I've investigated her in the past week, and I can find no evidence of her existence, beyond the court documents of Brock's trial, the newspaper clippings about the murder, and my own notes.

It's not entirely uncommon for an immigrant to be untraceable. Not all of them come here through the proper channels or with adequate documentation. The fact that she does not exist on paper does grant a level of circumstantial credibility to Brock's claim, however.

In response to this, and to my general curiosity and obsession, I conducted another act of lucid dreaming last night. It was my goal to return to that nameless city and take something back to the real world with me, just as Brock claimed to do with the McNaught woman. My previous attempts had failed, but I was learning from Brock. I was more in tune with the dreamlands than I had ever been.

Laying down to enter sleep, I tried to relieve myself of the lenses that Brock said blurred my vision. I cleared my mind of theory and jargon—those things on which I most prided myself for my knowledge. I tried my best to table my ambitious thoughts—my desire to see my name among psychiatric luminaries—the practical and material advantages that might be exploited by gifts such as Brock's. Focusing on the stuff of dreams—beauty and awe and desire, I closed my eyes.

I found myself, almost immediately, in front of the door from the Albright painting. It was different from the artist's interpretation. The color was slightly off, and I remembered what Brock had said about the tone of the wood being such that he had never seen the color anywhere else. The wreath writhed like woven serpents and the flowers looked insubstantial, as if their petals were made from colored mist. Still, it was unmistakably the inspiration behind that wonderful piece of art.

The dimensions of the door were impossible and contradicting. At first glance It was immeasurably tall, stretching into the black heavens, its wreath like a knot of redwoods. Yet as I approached, I found the door small enough for me to reach the knob and it pushed open with ease. This, interestingly, was the inverse of Brock's experience.

Across the threshold was the nameless, ruined city. My skin glowed in the silver radiance of the moons, and pinpricks of black starlight freckled my body. I walked slowly across the uneven rubble and the sunken stone-paved roads, toward the shattered remains of the hillside temple. The faceless monoliths on either side of the sacred ruins glared at me without expression, as if they knew I had come as a thief.

Walking between those stone sentries, I feared they might come to life, and clobber me with limestone fists, but they did not stir. Artifacts showed in the temple's wreckage—bits of gold and polished jewels. A copper censor, patinated to a soft green, lay half-buried, beside stone tablets with eroded carvings.

I dared not take anything of too great value, as I feared attracting the attention of the faceless monoliths. Instead, I retrieved a piece of leaded glass from the ground. It was long and thin, like a crystal dagger. I wondered for a moment if this was by design. Had it been a tool of sacrifice? Some wicked instrument used in unholy rites? Or was it simply a scrap of refuse?

Holding it above for closer examination, the shard took on the amber color of the sky, mottled with black dots from the unlight of dark stars. A barely perceptible silver sheen radiated from the glass, as if it was surrounded by a halo of moonlight. It seemed lighter in my hand, like empty air. Conversely, there was an enormous weight to it, which I felt in my soul.

I palmed the shard of glass, gripping it tightly. Its razor-sharp edge cut into my flesh and my blood dripped onto the ruins of the temple. I focused on the pain and urged my body to wake. A sound like thunder and grinding stone echoed through the dead city. I knew that I had awoken the faceless guardians, but I dared not look upon them. Instead, I pressed harder against the glass, determined to hold on to it, and reached for my physical body, so far away.

My eyes flew open, and my heart thundered in my chest. I was in my bed, in the real world, and in my hand was a long sliver of yellow glass, stained with black pinpricks, and slick with my blood.

Vinke, Brock - Session 7
November 27, 1951

I showed Brock the artifact that I stole from the dream. I realize it doesn't qualify as evidence to anyone else—just a bit of yellow glass—but Brock recognized it at once for what it was.

"I warned you not to take from your sleep. Something bad happens to dreams here. They get bent and broken. They turn ugly."

"It's just a piece of glass," I responded, holding it up to the light in my office. "Maybe it turns dull or loses its color. What does it matter?"

"You think you stole a piece of glass? Some rubbish from the ground?" Brock shook his head, something akin to a smirk on his lips. "Look closer, Doc. You stole the sky."

The shard gave off a silver radiance, despite its amber tone, and despite the yellow glow of the incandescent lights in my office. Thin black shadows, like negative starlight, stretched out from the black dots on the glass.

"My god," I heard myself mutter. "I did steal the sky"

"I ran off with something as simple as love and look how badly that went," Brock droned. "I'm glad I won't be here to see how this turns out."

"Won't be here?" I turned my attention to my patient, my concern returning to him, rather than my preoccupations.

"I think I'm done with this place, Doc. I'm tired of living in two worlds. You've helped me see that. Thank you."

"What do you mean, Brock?"

"This whole world—the one that everyone thinks is real—it's made up of stolen dreams, but dreams don't belong here. That's why everything turns to shit. Towers crumble. Marriages go to hell. Movements become wars."

"That doesn't mean we just give up," I countered.

"I'm not giving up. I'm just going home. I returned what I stole. I gave Kerrigan back, and now I can go home"

"Will you simply kill yourself the way you killed the McNaught girl? Is that what you mean? Do you think that will get you there?"

He didn't answer. His gaze was locked on the painting of the door.

"You may have a connection to the realm of dreams, but this is your home, Brock. You're a real person made of flesh and blood."

"This place isn't home for any of us. We're all dreams, doc. Every child ever born started as a dream, and most of us end up as nightmares."

"That's not true."

"Isn't it? Look 'round this place. Lonely bookworms, trying to fix broken men and women with drugs and fancy words. Worlds that make sense, don't need lunatic asylums."

### Vinke, Brock - Post-mortem entry
### December 1, 1951

Brock Vinke is gone. I have called this a post-mortem entry, but that's not entirely accurate.

After our last session, I put Brock on suicide watch. I had feared that he might take his own life as a conceived means of escape into the dream world. My concern in this regard was based upon his statements in our last session, as well as the crime which brought him to Danvers—the murder of Kerry McNaught.

I couldn't sleep that night. Even in those moments of restless slumber, I had no dreams. As such, I rose early and went to check on Brock. I found his room empty and unattended. After berating one of the orderlies who had been tasked with keeping watch over him, the orderly informed me that he had no idea what or who I was talking about.

I won't bother going into all the details here, but after going on a tirade to several other staff members, I found that none of them had any recollection of Brock Vinke or even a man of his description ever being admitted here. The absurdity of such claims forced me to pull out

Brock's files and records, but there were none to be had. The only papers I could find were my notes on our sessions. Even the court documents and newspaper clippings regarding the murder of Kerry McNaught were missing.

Ironically enough, I next went to the patients looking for validation of my sanity. Out of all the patients, only Mr. Schraft recalled Brock, and he remembered him only as a nightmare ...a hulking brute who punished him in his dreams.

I have since taken a leave of absence. It seems prudent to put aside some time to make sense of Brock and his disappearance. I need to step back, and more fully understand my own preoccupation with the dreamlands. I feel that I'm so close to understanding that realm—to finding attunement with the collective unconscious of all mankind. I know I was close, but my connection has crumbled like dried sand. I can't even fall asleep anymore, never mind reach the vistas of unreality that so enthrall me.

The amber dagger of glass that I stole from the ruined dream city is gone as well. It vanished the night Brock disappeared and in its place was a piece of sea glass, roughly the same shape, but its edges and color both worn dull. At first, I thought that Brock had stolen my find, perhaps to return it to the temple grounds I had stolen it from. As night fell and the sky turned from gray to muddy yellow, and then to burnished gold, I realized that the truth was much worse.

I stand now, beneath two moons, each so much larger than the one I have known all my life. Their silver radiance lends a soft glow to the thin and wispy clouds that share the amber heavens with ebony stars. The familiar constellations have abandoned the heavens. Gone is Orion with his shield and club, as well as his hunting dog. In their places, far-flung black suns line up in the shape of devils upon the heavenly canvas.

The unlight of those dark stars changes what it touches. Skin goes pallid and veins turn dark. Grass becomes brittle and soil hardens like clay. I think of Brock's warnings, that the waking world corrupts all dreams, and I wonder what terrible futures await us beyond the alien horizon.

No one else remembers the sky as it was. They cannot fathom a world with a single moon. I'm thought mad when I speak of black nights and white stars or powder blue heavens that awaken each morning.

Tonight, I will try to dream again, but the door has been closed to me since the night I robbed the hillside temple in that nameless city. I press my hands upon it, but it is as impossibly heavy as it is tall.

Will I ever be able to return? Will I ever sleep again? Brock said he was able to go home after returning what he had stolen. But how does one return the sky?

END

# ABOUT CURTIS M. LAWSON

CURTIS M. LAWSON is an author of unapologetically weird and transgressive fiction, fantastical graphic novels, and dark poetry. His work ranges from technicolor pulp adventures to bleak cosmic horror.

Curtis is a member of the Horror Writer's Association, and the host of the Wyrd Transmissions podcast. He resides just outside of Providence, RI.

# ABOUT JOSHUA REX

JOSHUA REX is an American author and historian. He was born in Sandusky, Ohio, and grew up between the Midwest and New England. He is the author of the novel A Mighty Word (Rotary Press) and the collections The Descent and Other Strange Stories (Weird House Press) and What's Coming for You (Rotary Press), and hosts the podcast The Night Parlor where he interviews authors, artists, historians, and musicians.

# ABOUT LUKE SPOONER

**Luke Spooner / Carrion House** is a freelance illustrator from the South East of England. Since graduating from Portsmouth University with a First-Class degree in illustration Luke has gone on to work on a wide variety of projects and commissions, including; illustrations and covers for horror, science fiction and fantasy books, magazines, graphic novels, conceptual design, CD packaging and business branding. Luke has also illustrated children's' books for authors who aim to promote diversity and mindfulness in younger audiences.

Notable projects for his darker, 'Carrion House' style of work have included stories by Neil Gaiman and Clive Barker as part of 'Gutted: Beautiful Horror Stories' and 'Behold: Oddities Curiosities and Undefinable Wonders,' both released through Crystal Lake Publishing. He also provided artwork for two stories by Stephen King; one through 'You, Human,' released through Dark Regions Press and another through 'Gamut Magazine.' Luke also acts as the illustrator for every instalment of Jay Wilburn's ongoing 'Dead Song' series of books.

**https://carrionhouse.com**